Christmas 2012

1—

to A. W. M. L —
with all my love
C/ G. +O

A DOG NAMED CHRISTMAS

DOUBLEDAY

New York London Toronto Sydney Auckland

A Dog Named

CHRISTMAS

❄

GREG KINCAID

DOUBLEDAY

Published in the United States by Doubleday, an imprint of The Doubleday Publishing Group, a division of Random House, Inc., New York. www.doubleday.com

DOUBLEDAY is a registered trademark and the DD colophon is a trademark of Random House, Inc.

Book design by Elizabeth Rendfleisch

Library of Congress Cataloging-in-Publication Data

Kincaid, Gregory D., 1957–
A dog named Christmas / by Greg Kincaid.—1st ed.
p. cm.
1. Youth with mental disabilities—Fiction. 2. Parent and adult child—Fiction. 3. Fathers and sons—Fiction. 4. Human–animal relationships—Fiction. 5. Family—Fiction. 6. Domestic fiction.
I. Title.
PS3561.I42526D64 2008
813'.54—dc22
2008004649

ISBN 978-0-385-52598-5

PRINTED IN THE UNITED STATES OF AMERICA

5 7 9 10 8 6 4

This book was always for my wife.
She has taught me so much,
not the least of which
is the value of a good dog.

A DOG NAMED CHRISTMAS

*J*ake seemed content with the Conner family, but even so, his departure was predictable. Mr. and Mrs. Conner lived on the edge of a growing city where subdivisions turned into ten-acre lots and where all too often people discarded beer cans, fast-food debris, and unwanted pets. Jake walked on, scruffy and half starved, with no tags. Mr. Conner found him resting on the back porch as an early February wind piled snow high on the drive-way of their modest ranch home. They fed him, cleaned and vaccinated him, and then just waited. They put up "Lost Dog" flyers, but no one called.

A walk-on like Jake has a different status than a pet you purchase. A walk-on can just as easily walk off, the Conners told each other.

The weeks passed and Jake stayed. Mr. and Mrs. Conner did not understand why anyone would dump him. Though the vet had confirmed he was a little bit older, he was one of the more engaging dogs they had known. With an alert personality, he was eager to please, house-trained, well behaved, and could sit, stay, and roll over on command. He was a good companion, keeping close without intruding, and was also curious and a quick learner.

Jake lingered through the summer, gaining weight and confidence in his surroundings, but by early fall, when his strength had fully returned, he seemed restless, like a pioneer yearning for his own territory, and would wander off at night and stay out for days and once for an entire week. He began roaming farther and farther away. The Conners tried fences and ties and even locking him up at night, but there were few bonds strong enough to keep him put for long. When the first frost collected on the still green grass and the moon was full, Jake left the Conner family to fulfill his own calling.

Speculation naturally followed. At the top of Mr. Conner's list was the assumption that Jake went home, back to wherever he came from. Mrs. Conner suggested that a wily female lured him away. The Conners' grown children wondered if Jake found a family with children to play with him, as their own children had when they visited their grandparents on weekends.

After the first few days, the Conners were concerned, but not alarmed. He was an important part of the family, but the Conners suspected that Jake operated by his own rules. As the days turned to weeks, and the weeks to months, his disappearance somehow seemed natural and the Conners just accepted his absence. A walk-on can walk off, they reminded themselves.

When they thought of him, they said things like, "He has Jake business to attend to. He'll come back if and when he is ready."

By the time winter came, Jake was like a faded old picture in a box of family memories. Occasionally at dinner, they would laugh and tell Jake stories, like the time a neighbor chased him down the middle of their driveway, trying to recover a twenty-pound black trash sack that dangled proudly from his jaws, or the time he chased a rabbit onto the frozen pond and spun around like an Olympic skater. The rabbit stopped and watched, seemingly laughing at Jake. Jake apparently thought it was fun too, for he backed up and did it again, with the same result.

Mrs. Conner would grow quiet as she felt his absence in her heart and then Mr. Conner would say, "Pass the potatoes . . . I'm sure he's fine."

When he left, Jake journeyed west away from the city and the Conners' home. It felt good to be a full-time roamer. He answered to no one. He had a freedom that few are brave enough to own. He slept beneath the stars, under bridges, in caves, in open fields tucked behind a log, or on the back porch of some generous soul who could tolerate a hobo on the road. He ate food that some might describe as unfit for a dog. He did what he needed to do to stay nourished. To do so, he honed the instincts lost to more modern times. He learned to listen, his sense of smell became more acute, and he noticed slight movements that would have gone undetected during his domestic life.

He hunted like an animal. He waited. He journeyed. He did not know how long it would take or how far he would go. It would be right when he got there. He had given himself over to instinct.

Like geese, salmon, and monarch butterflies, Jake was being pulled to a very particular place.

It was often dangerous. As he moved through less friendly neighborhoods, the residents had a way of making it clear that his kind was not wanted. They barely paid him a glance and were likely to pretend that he did not exist. They thought that showing him a little kindness would encourage him to stay and then they would never be rid of him.

If they were not ignoring him, they sent their hints in more obvious ways. One man threw a rock in his direction as he passed by. A carload of boys saw him walking on the side of the road one evening and they swerved in his direction as if it were funny to see him jump out of the way. Though Jake was unharmed, the message was clear. He needed to move on, keep heading west.

The animal kingdom was not generous toward him either. Dogs barked at him, skunks sprayed him, ticks bit him, and thorny bushes scraped at his sides. Still he kept going, aware that his journey was not yet complete.

These discomforts were minor inconveniences to Jake. He was content and at peace with himself. In the morning when he woke and stretched, his tired muscles felt good, never better. Hardship was the patina of his good life. There is no better state of mind for man or animal than being what you are and doing what you are meant to do. This harmony of existence and purpose is so rare that we forget it exists. Not Jake. Particularly, not today.

After the sun ascended to its midday vantage, Jake rested on a wooded knoll and watched as a young man in bright red tennis shoes wandered along a stream bank, aimlessly skipping rocks across the barely frozen surface of Kill Creek, bluntly named by the local Indians to suggest the abundance of wildlife that lived and died so near its banks.

As he watched the young man, the first thing he felt was a vague feeling of comfort and familiarity. Still, he cautiously waited, sensing that something was not quite right. After the man passed, he ambled down to the creek and drank deeply from the cool water that was yesterday's rainfall. There were smells that danced along the banks, like wildflowers, sweet hay, ancient oak, wet moss on limestone, and a strange, unfamiliar musky scent he could not place. He tried to separate the scent when he heard the slightest of sounds and spun around to see something, really only a blur, move away from him and into the deeper forest of hickory, walnut, red bud, and oak that flanked the creek.

He moved toward the woods and the scent grew stronger. Within a few moments, he found the tracks and made the connection. They were cat tracks. Enormous cat tracks. This was an engagement he did not want. He would not wait for the man to return. In the distance he could hear car engines, train whistles, dog barks, church bells, and the playful screams of children out for recess.

Jake stopped again and looked for the man in the bright red shoes and then moved toward the town sounds, hoping to find the thing for which he vaguely searched. Whatever it was that pulled him was growing stronger, persistent, and very near.

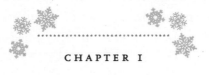

CHAPTER I

I spend more time now looking back than looking ahead, sifting through the years and pausing over the important events of my life. Maybe it's rare, but aside from the occasional sadness that accompanies us all, there is no litany of disappointments for me. Instead, there is a storehouse of good memories and special times. We all have some defining moments in our lives. Mine was a holiday that seemed perfect.

Of my five children, three boys and one daughter are grown and employed, but none is far away from this old farm we've called home for four generations. They come back for the holidays and sometimes for dinners, unsolicited advice, to borrow tools, or to just sit quietly on the porch with their feet propped up on the rail, listening to farm sounds, which lift our spirits even in the worst of times. They grew up here on land my great-great-grandfather purchased from the Blackfoot Indians. Just south of our house, a large stand of irises has spread over an acre of forest ground and hidden the remnants of his settler's cabin. Our memories on this farm are good.

Mary Ann, my wife, teaches English and debate at the Crossing Trails High School, from which each of the four generations of the McCray family have graduated. The more recent generations were spoiled by a school bus. The older two rode horses nearly eight miles each way and were not shy about recounting the details of their burdensome journey.

Then, there is Todd, my youngest child. By that Christmas he was old enough in years to be on his own, to have a real job like his siblings, but the immaturity that naturally accompanied his disability kept him home with his mother and me.

Todd looked like any other healthy twenty-year-old, but he had his own way of thinking about things. You'd know from watching or even talking with him briefly that something was unusual. Over the years, we tolerated some stares and whispers, but learned to think nothing of it. We loved and accepted everything about our youngest child, born to us later in life, a good ten years after we thought we were finished with diapers. Mary Ann, my wife of nearly forty years, frets over Todd and connects his problems with her late-life pregnancy.

I've learned that for every deficit one might see in Todd, there is an ability you don't see.

Todd always had his hands in his pockets and never seemed certain which direction he was going when he went out the door. His clothes seldom added up to an outfit and his hair, the color of sun-bleached rope, was punctuated with cowlicks and curls. Sometimes he would sit near a herd of sheep for an entire day, just watching. Other days, he would find a river and follow it upstream, searching for the place where the water began. He never found this place, but that did not deter him from trying.

Todd also loved to paint. If I stood him in front of a building, he would paint it. However, there was one problem. His mother was convinced that our son would forget he was on a ladder and fall straight off and hurt himself. He was under strict orders to climb no higher than the third rung, which left many painting projects half finished.

To add to this peculiar feature, our neighbors seemed to enjoy giving Todd their leftover paint. However kind this may have been, it did not result in a harmonious color scheme. Our farm was painted with colors rejected by others, often for good reasons. Once again, we grew accustomed to the staring, and no one laughed harder at it than we did. We always thought of it as primer over which we would someday paint, but, like most eyesores, in time we stopped noticing. We took great pride in telling passers-by that we were the Midwest testing site for the Todd Paint Company.

Unless it was something he felt passionate about, Todd usually wasn't much of a talker, but he whistled from memory, and off-key, every tune that he ever heard from his friend and constant companion, the radio. I continually pleaded with him to take off the earphones so I could talk to him. He gladly complied, but rarely would he take them off unless he was asked first.

The one thing that defined Todd's life more than any other was his relationship with animals. He held them, raised them, loved them, and laughed with them. I am outdoors caring for animals all day. When finished, I want to leave the work behind, so I try to keep animals out of my house, but if one could be carted, crated, boxed, or stalled, Todd tried to bring it into the barn or garage and, more times than not, sneak it up to his room. This worked well enough for squirrels, rabbits, and baby birds, but not so well for skunks, snakes, and toads. To make matters worse, Todd's room was always a mess, which served as an excellent camouflage for a variety of uninvited guests.

As he got older, Todd finally accepted that he would have to set wild animals free. Not to do so was cruel. The only exception was for creatures that were injured or otherwise unable to care for themselves. As a result, every hurt, maimed, and lost animal within five counties somehow made its way directly to our back porch.

There was no money for veterinarians, so Todd became a bit of an animal medicine man. He was not at all shy about using the phone to ask for help. In fact, I often had to work hard to keep him off it.

He was very patient and determined in his rescue missions. And it was rare for anyone to turn Todd down because they were too busy. It wasn't that they felt sorry for him. He was one of those people who could capture you with his enthusiasm, and before you knew it his urgent need became your urgent need.

He would set out calling Jim Morton, our vet, who in turn would give Todd the number of the U.S. Department of Agriculture or the National Park Service, depending on whether Todd's latest patient walked, climbed, flew, or slithered. One could amble into the room and find Todd talking to a professor of ornithology at the local university about a broken bird wing. Before long, it seemed like the entire American university system had abandoned world hunger and quantum physics. After all, there was the problem of Todd's bird that needed immediate attention.

Todd had a way of setting things in motion, and when he did, we dropped everything. I must admit, however, that I did not see this one coming.

One early December afternoon, Todd came running into the barn carrying his radio and frantically trying to scribble down a phone number. He handed me the wrinkled note.

"It's for a Christmas dog," he said.

"Slow down, Todd. What are you talking about?"

"The animal shelter wants you to adopt a dog for the Christmas holiday."

"Todd, they always want you to adopt a dog. That's what they do. Besides, we don't need another animal around here, and most definitely not a dog." We had been a dogless farm for many years, and I was not ready to change that arrangement. I had my own reasons for not wanting a dog—long-standing ones. It ended poorly with the last several dogs I let into my life and I was dead set against trying it again. I'd spent twenty years saying no to Todd's brothers and his sister and I saw no reason to change my mind now.

"It's just for Christmas," he said in what came as close to an argumentative tone as Todd could muster. "After that, you can take the dog back if you want. They have lots of dogs that don't have homes."

I pushed the scrap of paper into the front pocket of my jeans and hoped he would forget about it. But Todd continued with his innocent persistence that wore on you, yet was endearing. "Can I call them?" he pleaded as I tried to walk away.

"Todd, there is no use in calling. We've had this discussion before. We are not having a dog on this farm. We already have plenty of animals to care for. We don't need more. We've got work to do now." He was still looking disappointed. I wanted to give him time to adjust to a situation that he might have a hard time accepting. "Let's get some chores done and maybe we can talk about it later."

"It'll be too late by then. It will be closed and all the dogs will be gone." His voice quivered. He kicked at the earth with his large feet and hung his head. I knew he was only moments away from tears. Saying no to Todd was *never* easy.

I took the red handkerchief that I kept in my front overalls pocket and wiped the sweat from my brow. Just like the rest of us, it was sometimes difficult for Todd to accept that he could not always have what he wanted. It would take time to walk him through this one. I playfully grabbed him in a headlock and rubbed my knuckles across the crown of his head until he started to laugh, then I released my hold and held him by the lapels of his jacket and said, "Come on, Todd, let's go finish the chores and then we'll talk about it more tonight. Those dogs aren't going anywhere, and if they did, that would be a good thing for them."

We had a ritual of chores that started with the chickens, passed a hog or two, and ended up at a corral where I kept cows and their calves. We, of course, fed and watered the stock, but beyond that, without ever thinking about it, we made sure each animal was healthy. You can't take a chicken's temperature and cattle don't sneeze when they're sick. You have to sense something is wrong, usually by the way they move or don't move.

Todd slipped between the rails of the corral and walked freely among the cows, touching and assessing each animal that he passed. Cattle and sheep are less domesticated than horses and don't generally like to be handled or touched, which made Todd's ability unusual. I watched him as he made his rounds and called out updates.

"The twins look good."

"Yeah, they do," I answered back.

"Old Two Stubs looks thin. Do you think we should worm her again?"

"Probably," I concurred, readying a mixture of corn and sorghum to pour into a long cylindrically shaped aluminum trough. The calves bawled as the larger cows jostled for a front-row seat. There are no manners in the feedlot. The biggest always win.

Todd stopped in his tracks as if he remembered something important. Surrounded by hungry, jostling animals but without the least bit of fear, he worked his way out of the corral. He closed the distance between us and then stood six inches from my face and just stared at me. I had no idea what was on his mind.

"What?" I finally asked.

"The cows are fine, Dad."

"So?"

"Could I call—now?"

"Todd Arthur McCray, enough about the dogs. Okay?"

He frowned and walked toward the house. Todd was such a good kid, but I needed more time to think about this one. If I decided against it, Todd was going to find it difficult to accept, but I knew I should not let disappointing Todd get in the way of making the right decision.

Truth was that I missed having a dog, but there were a lot of reasons to move slowly on this one. Certainly, it would make Todd and his mother happy. In fact, I knew darn well that if I let Todd or his mother so much as look at a dog, it would own the farm by sunset and I'd be lucky even to have a place at the dinner table. I could picture the chaos that would ensue.

"Where's your father, Todd? I don't believe I've seen him for two or three years now."

"What do you mean, Mom? Dad is still here. He's been out on the back porch for the last couple of winters. You know, where you put him after we got the dog."

"Oh, yes, I remember now."

"Todd, get the dog and come to dinner, we're having prime rib. You know how Fido just loves prime rib. If there is any left over, put it out on the back porch for your dad and do tell him hello for me the next time you see him."

When it was time for dinner, or what my grandfather called supper, I walked past the porch on the south side of our home and into the mudroom at the back of the house. I sat on a bench and took off my muddy boots and overalls. I could hear Todd and Mary Ann talking at the kitchen table. He had started dog campaigning with his mother. As I expected, it took very little convincing. To her credit, she waited at least ten or fifteen seconds before she sold me down the river.

"Yes, Todd, I can see why you want the dog, and no, I don't understand why he would not want you to have one. Like you said, it's just for a week and then you can take the dog back if it doesn't work out for you. I heard the whole thing on the radio and it seems like such a nice thing to do for those poor dogs."

"I would take good care of him, Mom."

"Of course you would, Todd. Your dad knows that too. We'll just have to work on him, won't we?"

"Is there some reason I shouldn't have the dog?" I heard him ask.

"None. None at all," she said.

The discussion I wanted to have with Todd had just occurred in my absence. Our home is not a democracy. It is a benevolent dictatorship. Queen Mary Ann had spoken.

From the mudroom bench I stood up and walked into the kitchen, took off my leather gloves, set them on the kitchen counter, and jumped into the conversation. "I know there are lots of reasons to give this dog program a try, but I still am not sure that it's a good idea."

Todd was not too worried about my concerns. "The radio said it was a good idea."

"Yes, I'm sure the radio thinks it's a good idea, but still I want to check into it myself. Can you two wait for me to do that?" I asked.

"Yes," Todd said with no conviction.

I smiled at him and said, "Hard time waiting, huh?"

"Can't wait."

"Big rush?"

He knew I was teasing him and he smiled back and said, "Can't wait."

"They're closed tonight. Do you think we should call the emergency number to check on this program or could you and your mother hold off until morning to discuss this further?"

He paused and it was clear that he was seriously considering calling the emergency number. "Todd!" I said.

He pondered his options and finally said, "I guess I can wait."

That night, after Todd went to bed, the dog issue was discussed further. "Mary Ann, I am willing to consider the Christmas dog program, but I need more details."

I took a deep breath and continued on to a more sensitive subject. "The way you handled this whole thing with Todd irritated me."

"I have absolutely no idea what you are talking about," she said with the innocence of a spring lamb. This was a diversionary strategy the debate coach saved for those rare occasions when she knew I was right.

"Todd and I needed to talk about the program together. Reach an understanding about this. You know, have a discussion."

"Did I stop you from having that discussion?" she asked, knowing full well that she was avoiding the real issue.

"By the time I entered the room, you and Todd were pouring puppy chow in a steel bowl and you know it." I did not enjoy confronting my wife, but I was quite sure that what she had done was not fair.

"George, what are you talking about? I never did any such thing. I was just acknowledging Todd's feelings. You just need to admit that you cannot say no to Todd and please do not blame me for your inability to be tough with him."

I recognized a sly switching of gears in her attack. "What are you talking about?" I asked with an accusing tone in my voice.

"I am tired and I am going to bed. Perhaps tomorrow we can have a more civil discussion on this subject. I do not feel like being yelled at and unfairly accused." My wife pushed her nose to the ceiling in mock indignation and left the room. I had seen this act before and there was no way I was going to fall for it this time.

I followed her into the living room. "You know I'm right, don't you?"

Cornered, she had to concede the point. "Well, perhaps I did give in a little too quickly."

"Five seconds?" I asked.

"I tried to make it to ten." Mary Ann then switched tactics again and said what was really on her mind. "Oh, George, why can't you just let Todd have the dog?"

"You know why, Mary Ann."

"I don't mean to be insensitive, but your bad dog history was a long time ago. Believe me, you would be better off to forget about it and try again."

"I'll think about it," I grumbled, and went into another room, sat in a chair, and rested my face in my hands and tried to think about something I didn't like to think about—my history of dog experiences.

When I was twelve years old my father was killed in a tractor accident and his parents—my grandparents—moved back into our house. Not knowing what else to do for me, my grandfather came home one day with an Irish setter. I grew up with the world's best dog, Tucker. No other kids lived near our farm, so Tucker became my best friend. We hunted, explored, and understood each other. No rabbit, quail, rattlesnake or prairie chicken was safe from me and Tucker.

He somehow got me through what would have otherwise been a very lonely adolescence.

After I graduated from high school, the United States Army gave me a one-year, all-expenses-paid Vietnam vacation. Tucker, now an old man of a dog, patiently waited for me on the back porch for months, just like I was going to come home from football practice any minute. My grandmother wrote to me on April 7, 1969, to tell me that Tucker died on the back porch waiting for me to come home. His collar and tags still hang from an ancient nail in our barn. I missed him, but given where I was, I just moved ahead and tried to stay alive.

In June 1969, our patrol made its way into a village. The last and only living thing left was a half-starved dog of indeterminate breed. It was against regulations, but I kept that dog with me for the next four months. I hoped he would replace the empty space that came from being so far away from home and losing Tucker. We made him our platoon mascot and, after considering several worthy nominations, settled on the name "Good Charlie." He became my new best friend and the only sane and kind creature in a part of the world filled with brutality. He saved my life, but it cost him his own when he bounded ahead of me and stepped on a land mine.

It took me a very long time to get over grieving for

Tucker and maybe even longer for Good Charlie. Not just because I missed the dogs, but also because they became important landmarks in my journey through the ugly war memories that are hard to shed. I still don't talk about either dog. Not even to Mary Ann. Some people may think I'm a dog grouch, but it isn't that simple.

I wanted to leave memories of guns and dogs back in Southeast Asia. My grandfather insisted that it was not safe to be on a farm without a rifle, so I kept his, a World War I .30-06 with five bullets, buried deep in my closet. Though I knew how to load and fire the old gun, I hoped it would never be needed. My dog memories were buried even deeper. People wonder why I don't have dogs on the farm. I let them wonder. Another dog was likely to bring back a flood of dark feelings, of losses and pain and lives cut short.

Deep in thought, I did not hear Mary Ann enter the living room. She startled me slightly with a hand on my shoulder. "George?" she asked.

"Yes," I said, without looking up.

"I'm sorry. We can forget about it this year. I should not have put you in this position. It was insensitive of me." She paused and then added, "I'll tell Todd that this is a bad year and we'll consider it next year. Maybe you'll be ready by then."

I reached out and held her hand. "No, Mary Ann, you're right. It's been almost forty years. That's long enough. It's time for me to get over this."

"Are you sure?"

"Yes, but there are still a few concerns I want to discuss."

"Like what?" she asked, without pushing.

"At the end of the week, we take the dog back. It's a one-week experiment. A nice thing to do for the holidays. Nothing more."

"Yes, George, I understand. That's how the program works. If you want to take the dog back, you can."

"You'll support me on this?"

"Of course I will. What else?"

"I want Todd to handle this responsibly. He feeds him and takes him out for walks, not you or me. Also, I think this is the perfect opportunity to get him to clean his room. No clean room, no dog."

"I agree," she said.

"Settled?" I asked.

"Done," she said.

I was inclined to give it a try. I felt better having an understanding with my wife. We had learned long ago that all couples fight, or at least argue from time to time. Mary Ann likes to say that it's not conflict itself, but unresolved conflict, that causes problems in life and marriage.

She grew up the daughter of the local banker and I wondered if getting everything she wanted as a child made it harder for her to say no to Todd. While I was in Vietnam, Mary Ann received her teacher's degree from Kansas State University. Between homework assignments, she wrote to me every day, and she was ready to marry me when I returned, shot up and crippled as I was. I quipped, "You only want me for my disability pension."

"That makes us even, George."

"Why's that?"

"You only want me for my teacher's salary."

I never questioned Mary Ann's sense of loyalty. She promised to be the best wife and the best mother any woman could be. She never let me down. We just did not always see things exactly the same way when it came to Todd.

This was going to be one of those occasions.

CHAPTER 2

The next morning, Todd was dressed and in the kitchen earlier than usual, trying to keep his excitement under control. After breakfast, Todd and I made our way through the corral and down to the barn. I took out the scrap of paper with the number on it and picked up the phone extension that I kept on the south barn wall. From the barn, I could call the shelter without any interference from Crossing Trail's debate coach.

A hundred reasons for not making that call raced through my mind, but I dialed the number anyway and tried my hardest to forget each and every one of them. At some level, I suspected that Todd and Mary Ann were right. However uncomfortable it might make me, it wouldn't hurt me to have a dog around the house for a week.

Todd's life was hard. It seemed that every day we had to

choose between trying to make his life better or just accepting that there were things in his world that we weren't big enough to change. Like the Christmas dog, the choices were not always easy.

The fact that Todd came to us so late in our lives sometimes made raising him more difficult. Every doctor we visited came up with a different diagnosis. I believe most were trying very hard to avoid telling us that Todd was mildly retarded. It's an ugly-sounding word. Nobody likes to say it. So, we heard *autism, learning disabled*. We heard *prenatal stroke, developmental delay, epilepsy,* and probably more. Truth was he just did not function at a high level. An exact diagnosis really didn't matter that much to me. All the doctors agreed that Todd would never get better.

He may have struggled at T-ball, soccer, and spelling bees, but we loved him and accepted him just the way he was, so what difference did it make? He needed us and we needed him—perhaps, even more.

Todd enriched our lives in countless ways, teaching us kindness, acceptance, and patience in a thousand little daily lessons. We came to understand what a special gift he was to us. When Todd was born, we vowed never to allow "I'm tired" or "I'm too old" to get in the way of doing what needed to be done for him.

I reminded myself of this vow as I dialed the phone.

"Cherokee County Animal Shelter," said a voice from the other end of the line. "This is Hayley."

I suspected that it was Hayley Donaldson, a former student of Mary Ann's and classmate of my daughter's. Clearing my throat to bring my mind back to the task at hand, I responded, "Hayley, this is George McCray. My son Todd is interested in something he heard on the radio about a Christmas dog."

"Oh, yeah, you're Hannah's dad, right?"

"That's right."

"What can I tell you?"

"Todd's given me a few details, but I want to make sure he understands." I glanced over at my boy. His eyes were beaming. And although it warmed me to the core to see him this happy, I was already getting an uneasy feeling about adopting a dog.

"Over the holidays, many of us like to do kind things for other people," Hayley began. "At the shelter, we offer animal lovers an opportunity to extend that holiday spirit to an animal. You come by anytime from around December eighteenth on and pick out your dog. You keep him until at least the twenty-sixth. We're pretty flexible on the dates. We're more concerned that the Adopt a Dog for Christmas program works for your family and that you have a good time with our dogs. You feed him and give him lots of attention, then bring the dog back if you want. Otherwise, our dogs stay in a three-foot-by-six-foot steel cage for the holidays. At this time of year, with so much of our staff off, there just isn't time to do much more than give an occasional pat on the head."

I raised my voice slightly for Todd's benefit and then

carefully asked, "There is no obligation to keep the dog, right?"

"Absolutely not."

"Are there enough volunteers?" I realized the question was absurd.

"No, Mr. McCray. There are never enough volunteers. It seems that we always have more dogs than good homes for them."

I could see how Adopt a Dog for Christmas might work for us, but many questions still ran through my head. Was this just a scheme for the shelter's employees to get a few days off? How could the dogs possibly know that it was Christmas? Wasn't this a holiday for humans? Would I feel guilty when I returned the dog? Would Todd understand and accept the transitory nature of the program?

Ultimately, it was one of the times in my life when I took a deep breath and trusted that it would work. I was never one who believed that the road to hell is paved with good intentions. In fact, I believed just the opposite to be true.

"We'll come and take a look," I said, suppressing a sigh of reluctance.

"That's great. If you decide to adopt a dog for the holidays, there is some paperwork, but we know your family, so it's really just a formality."

"Thanks, Hayley. We'll see you in a couple of weeks."

Todd was obviously pleased that I made the call. He smiled, nodded his head, and walked away from the barn to conduct the latest in his series of painstaking experiments to determine just how well paint adheres in December. I assumed that after seven years on this experiment, Todd Paints was on the verge of releasing the shocking results of this research to the public: Paint does not adhere particularly well, or spread with ease, when it's nearly freezing outside.

It was cold for early December that year and we had an abnormally large amount of snow. Winter weather triggers pleasant memories for me. My grandfather had a very important job in Cherokee County. He drove a maintainer, or what we might call a grader today. The title of County Road Maintainer, which was only slightly less prestigious than "Your Honor," was bestowed upon him. At first, the maintainer was pulled by two large draft horses, named Dick and Doc. They were lavishly housed in giant box stalls in our barn. Later, the county acquired a maintainer that was powered by a diesel engine that was extraordinarily reliable.

It was my grandfather's job to keep the gravel roads graded in the summer and clear of snow in the winter. When I was a boy, a big snowstorm would cause our family to spring into action with tremendous urgency.

My grandmother would make coffee and put it into an old thermos. I could tell by the smell of the pot brewing in the predawn hours that it was a snow day. She would make up a sack of sandwiches and cookies large enough to feed my grandfather for several meals straight.

In the middle of the night, Bo McCray would start up that old grader. It would loudly spew and spat, daring the snow to fall, and then shoot balls of sparks into the dark snow-stained sky like a mighty titan awakening from a deep, centuries-old slumber. I liked the sound of the mammoth machine coming to life. Eventually the engine would smooth out and I could hear him pull out of the driveway, heading the maintainer west toward town. I would listen until the sound was gone, picturing the snow pushed aside effortlessly.

This was one of those familiar childlike images where we see adults towering above us with inconceivable power and ability. Eventually the roar of the maintainer disappeared into the night, but it left me with good thoughts about my grandfather moving all of that snow out of the way as I snuggled deep down into sheets of flannel and blankets of wool.

The heat from the wood furnace did not make it to the edges of the house that were relegated to the children. A glass of water set on my bedside table was likely to have ice in it by the early morning hours, but it somehow mattered less because I knew that the roads were clear and each day held endless possibilities, including a very good chance of a school-closing decision made after the school consulted with my grandfather, who was often kind enough to ask my opinion.

Sometimes Grandfather McCray would work twenty-four, or even thirty-six, hours straight, plowing snow. When he grew tired, my father would climb onto the maintainer and take a shift, and when I got older, after my father died,

I took my turn. I loved the feeling of clearing the snow, and the admiration of our neighbors was considerable.

The elderly, sick, or poor were likely to wake and find their own private driveways also cleared of snow—a brief detour my grandfather was sure the county could afford.

Our lives depended on my grandfather maintaining the roads. Many homes did not have phones to call for help and what phone service did exist was unreliable and frequently lost in bad weather. Without the roads cleared, there was tremendous isolation.

Over the Christmas holidays, we were the most popular people in Cherokee County, Kansas. Around four o'clock on the Sunday afternoon before Christmas, my grandmother and my mother would make a large pot of oyster stew, cook a ham, and make an enormous bowl of mashed potatoes. Aunt Elizabeth brought her famous cinnamon rolls and cherry pie, which my cousins and I fought over as if they were lost pirate treasure.

Around seven o'clock on that same Sunday evening, our neighbors showed their gratitude by dropping by with Christmas cookies, gifts, or homemade ornaments to string on our tree. Because we expected the company, my mother, and now many years later Mary Ann, made our old farmhouse seem like the Midwest regional office for Claus Enterprises. Half of our basement was filled with gifted decorations and no one dared, now or then, to throw away one piece of worn-out holly. Every ornament had earned a spot. Whether it was true or not, we expected that each neighbor and friend was closely watching to make sure their ornaments had earned a place in our decorating scheme.

As the years passed, the neighbors came by not to thank my grandfather for removing snow but to see the Christmas decorations at the McCray house that had evolved and been added to for generations. Our house was a museum of Christmas treasures past and present. The Sunday before Christmas family dinner and open house was a very special part of our holiday tradition.

It had always been my job to hang the lights, but on this day I had a helper. Todd, who of course could not come up the ladder, stood below, headphones on under his stocking cap, and handed me the lights. As I strung them around the house, the sun hid behind patchy clouds and little independent flakes of snow occasionally fluttered to the ground. Although our house is modest, it takes me more than two hours to do the lights.

When Todd and I finished the outside lights, we went to the basement and started the trek up and down the stairs carrying boxes. My wife is very organized and each box is labeled with a destination. For Todd it was like rediscovering forgotten toys.

Mary Ann would spend hours with Todd over the coming weeks hanging and recounting the history of our Yuletide treasure trove.

CHAPTER 3

As the holiday approached, Todd and I began to make a game out of the Christmas dog.

"We get the dog on the eighteenth and when do we return him?" I asked Todd.

"Dog goes back on the twenty-sixth."

"When does Christmas end, Todd?"

"Christmas ends on the twenty-sixth, Dad—and that's when the dog has to go back to the shelter."

I put my arm around Todd's shoulder and hugged him. "That's good, Todd. We're going to have fun with the Christmas dog, aren't we?"

With all of the work helping his mother to decorate the house and cleaning his own room, Todd was pleased to see Christmas week arrive. He removed at least six large trash sacks of junk from his room and I kept making him clean more while I had his attention. Neither his mother nor I dared to look into those sacks out of the sincerest fear of what had lurked in the dark folds of that boy's room. I'm sure he spent at least two full days on the project. When he thought it was clean, we had him mop the floor and wash the walls with warm soapy water. This might be our last opportunity to insist upon this level of cleanliness.

As I stood in the doorway and watched him work, I could hear Mary Ann laughing on the phone with one of her friends from Crossing Trails High School.

"I did not think I would ever see his room this clean. Not since the Lord fed five thousand with two fish and five loaves has anyone been able to make so much of so little. Todd can take one candy wrapper and in two hours manufacture an entire sack of trash. He can create clutter out of breeze and sunlight."

I turned back in Todd's direction as he said, "It's clean," holding a rag high in the air to signal the completion.

Wandering around the room grunting approval, I finally mustered the nerve to look under the bed. To my surprise, it was clean too. "This room is fit for a Christmas dog." He acknowledged his assent with a grin and I went back outside to work.

Todd probably had not slept much the last few nights leading up to December 18. He'd spent two weeks speculating to me about the kind, size, breed, and shape of the dog he wanted to adopt and this gave us both some opportunity to tease, which I gladly allowed.

"I think I want a big one," he said.

"Really," I said.

"Big like an elephant." Todd extended his arms as much as he could and still it was only slightly wider than his grin.

"An elephant would be real comfortable in your room. They like jungle."

"Not anymore, Dad. It's clean now."

"Considering all that junk you took out, maybe you could fit two elephants in there. Should we call the zoo and see if they have an elephant adoption program?"

"Dad, I don't want an elephant."

"Just a big dog. Right?"

"Of course, I could take three small ones instead."

"Perhaps," I fired back. "You could take one dog for a week or you could take three different dogs for one day each."

He stood there figuring for a few seconds and then smiled when he completed the math. "Nah, I think one big dog for a week is better."

When the eighteenth finally did arrive, Todd was at the breakfast table waiting for me, dressed and ready to go. I came down in my robe and slippers with a towel wrapped around my head, a rare sight for Todd.

"Mary Ann," I offered in my sickest and weakest voice, "I have a frightful headache—could be pneumonia. I'll have to spend the entire day in bed. We can only hope for a recovery before spring planting. You and Todd will have to do the chores for me till then."

She stood there with her hands on her hips and said, "Oh, George, quit teasing that boy. Get back up those stairs and change your clothes this minute!"

"I hurt too badly, Mary Ann." I tried to sniffle and hold back a few tears of pain. "I don't think I can walk." I stumbled into the living room and fainted on the couch. For extra effect, I stuck my one good leg vertically into the air and let it tremble with the last movements of life. My eyelids fluttered, my arms dropped limply to my sides, and I died on the spot.

Mary Ann followed me in and pulled the towel from around my head and said, "George, since you are so sick, maybe today would be a good day for Todd to practice driving the truck on his own. Can we have your keys?"

Springing back to life, I announced, "I'm feeling better. All I need is a good, hearty breakfast."

"Well, then, get in here and sit down and eat it before it gets cold," Mary Ann ordered.

At the table, I remembered my manners, and kindly commented on each and every bite of breakfast. "Mmmm, mmmm, Mary Ann, these are the finest pancakes you have ever made. Are there seconds? Thirds?"

"Same recipe for years now, George. You just eat 'em and quit talking about 'em."

"Anything different about this coffee? Sure tastes good."

"Nope and there is nothing different about this foot." She held her rigid right foot in the air in a menacing way. "Would you like to reacquaint yourself with it?"

I turned to Todd, who had sat through the entire meal wearing his hat, coat, and gloves, and said, "You about ready to go, son?"

"Yes. I am ready."

"Well, if you are ready, why are we sitting in this kitchen jawing with your mother? We have important work to do. Dog picking is today. Don't you remember that today is dog-picking day?"

He stood up and said, "Yes, we should go."

"Let me put on my best dog-picking clothes and then we'll leave."

I stood up from the table and before I could head upstairs to change, Todd gave me an enormous hug and the connection between the two of us seemed to run down through my toes.

Todd was generous with hugs and we did nothing to discourage them, even though they were sometimes offered at unexpected times and places. The school bus driver and the FedEx man both got used to them. There were other little social cues that Todd may have vaguely recognized but often ignored. Some of these Mary Ann worked hard to curb, like not leaving the bathroom door wide open so he could carry on a conversation with anyone within shouting distance. Other habits, like not keeping his room clean, we tolerated. Most boys stop holding their parents' hands when they turn nine or ten, but when we were alone and when he forgot just how old he was, Todd would grab Mary Ann's or my hand and walk along with us. This morning was special. It was not only a dog-picking day, but as we left the house for town, it was also a hugging and hand-holding day.

Walking toward the truck, I squeezed his hand gently.

My old brown Ford moved toward town at a pace that was too slow for Todd. Those size 12 red-sneakered feet tapped twice for each beat of the music that played on the truck's AM radio, and though he knew how long it took, he kept asking, "How much further, Dad?"

"At least another four or five days, Todd. You know what a long journey it is to town. We've got to cross the Rocky Mountains, pass through the Great Mojave Desert, go down one side and back up the other side of the Grand Canyon, and then loop all the way around Toledo." I paused and added, "And, 'cause I know you are in a hurry, I'm not factoring in a thing for tornadoes."

"Dad," he whined. "How much longer—really?"

"Ten minutes, son. Ten minutes."

Todd smiled contentedly, knowing just how close he was to the shelter.

"When do we take the dog back, Todd? Do you remember?"

"Yes, Dad, the dog goes back on the twenty-sixth. That's when Christmas ends."

"Very good. You know, if this goes well and if we all have fun and get the dog back to the shelter on time, maybe we could do it next year too. Would you like that?"

"Sure." Todd looked up at me with a smile. The last two

weeks had given me time to adjust to the idea, but most of all I was pleased to be doing this for him.

The sign on the edge of town proudly proclaims WELCOME TO CROSSING TRAILS—WHERE THE OREGON, SANTA FE, AND CALIFORNIA TRAILS ALL MEET. There is only one stoplight in Crossing Trails and it seemed to be unnecessary as we sat there alone waiting for the light to turn green.

A small police station about the size of a convenience store rests on one corner and the volunteer fire department is on another. Every year the two stations have a competition to see who can decorate their respective building with the most holiday flair. Perhaps because the fire station is manned by volunteers, over the last few years the town's Christmas Committee seemed partial to the cornerstone of their scheme: Santa at the helm of an antique horse-drawn fire engine. This year the police station countered with Santa's reindeer pulling an antique police car.

Main Street has seen little new construction over the years. All of the commercial structures, just to the ragged side of charming, are close to a hundred years old. Some of the buildings stubbornly cling to old wooden sidewalks cut from the durable oaks harvested from the nearby forests. Nearly all were decked out with holiday greenery and white Christmas lights.

Two blocks ahead and on the right side of the town square is the Cherokee County Courthouse. A bronze statue of a tired pioneer, hat in hand and staring west, stands at the base of the steps. An old gazebo commands the courthouse lawn and still serves as the home for the Cherokee County Volunteer Band, which would be performing their holiday program several times before Christmas, weather permitting.

Like many old things, the courthouse had remained antiquated long enough to become historic. A tall spire with a bell tower constructed of native limestone and brick rose high over the surrounding buildings. Judge Crawford, the county's only permanent judge, took a break in December from his duties.

In Crossing Trails, the farther you move away from the town square, the faster the charm wears off. Near the edge of town, after passing over the tracks for the old Atchison, Topeka and Santa Fe Railway, there is a trailer park and an old gravel road that leads south to the county fishing lake.

We turned and followed the gravel past poorly kept and poorly constructed homes, punctuated by even more poorly kept yards, littered with worn-out cars and rusted swing sets. The less fortunate make their homes on the South Side. At one point this was good farm ground, but the water treatment plant, a trailer court, and cheap rental housing had changed all of that for the worse. If I remembered correctly, Hayley's grandparents lived on this ground when it was still farmed. Now the South Side and the county animal shelter were places that most people (and all animals) preferred to avoid.

As I came around the last bend in the gravel road, and the shelter was in view, Todd unhooked his seatbelt. Before

I came to a full stop in the shelter's parking lot, marked with potholes like a mortar-littered battlefield, Todd threw open the truck door and headed toward the entrance. He moved quickly past an old Nissan pickup truck that Hayley drove. I recognized it as a car I often saw in town, usually with a few dogs in the back and another couple in the cab. The bumper sticker read, DOG ABUSERS SHOULD GET WHAT THEY GIVE.

There are several places that I prefer to not know too much about. Animal shelters are one of them. Our town's shelter, like most, was underfunded and crowded past capacity. Makeshift trailer annexes of critter cages filled with complaining felines were permanently parked next to the original building. The dingy yellow brick structure itself was discarded years ago by the sewer district. On warm days, when the wind came from the south, it became obvious why the county moved their administrative offices closer to town.

As soon as I had pushed the front door open, I realized that the interior of the shelter was only a slight improvement. The humans had given up their office space to make room for more animals and the reception area had become the administrative offices, so crammed with desks that one could barely pass without jostling papers or boxes that hung over the edges. Just past the reception area was the break room, where old reports and records, medicines, brochures, and books were stored. Against the wall of the break room was a worn-out countertop that the vet used for routine procedures and where a coffeemaker tried hard to crank out a pot of coffee one drip at a time.

Not seeing anyone in the front of the building, we moved through a swinging door, where we found dogs and considerable human activity.

As Todd and I walked into the large holding area, I was immediately struck by how clean the staff managed to keep the building and the cages. It must have taken a considerable effort. One dog started barking at us and soon more chimed in, like a symphony building to a crescendo. Before long, the entire population of maybe thirty-five dogs was whipped into a frenzy of barks, whines, and howls. A woman clanged a dinner bowl on the side of a metal cage, a sound that seemed to distract them and bring a halt to most of the noise. I recognized Hayley as she walked toward us. Her name tag confirmed my suspicion. She wore her prematurely graying hair in a long braid and dressed in blue jeans and a dusty green jacket.

"Hello, Hayley. Nice to see you again. We're here to adopt a dog for Christmas."

She reached out and took Todd's big hand in hers. After she held it for a moment and he did not respond as most adults would, by returning the shake and offering some salutation, she tilted her head slightly and looked into Todd's big brown eyes. Her face showed genuine affection and kindness.

"I'm Hayley. It's nice to meet you, Todd. I remember you from the county fair." It was as if she knew to look past his disability and speak directly to the enthusiastic boy inside this strong young man.

"Yes, I was in 4-H."

"I remember how nicely you handled your animals. I recall a few blue ribbons safety-pinned to your shirt one year not too long ago, right?"

"Yes, sheep and cattle." Todd was very involved in 4-H, but unfortunately he was now too old to participate. It had been a great confidence builder for him.

"Todd, I know you are an old hand with animals, so look over all of the dogs and then we'll decide together if there is a good fit for you and your family. The unadoptable dogs are quarantined. So, just look around and let me know if you need some help or have any questions." She reached out and held Todd's forearm for a moment, as if she wanted to say something else, but instead she just turned and walked away, busily moving from cage to cage—doing what, I was not sure.

Over the years, I had learned that you could tell a lot about a person simply based on the way they related to Todd. I had a good feeling about Hayley.

This was a very important decision for my son and I did not want to rush him. After finding a bench, I attempted to read a newspaper that someone had left behind while Todd walked up and down the rows of cages to find just the right companion for Christmas. The floor had recently been washed and the smell of chlorine bleach hung in the air along with various animal odors. My ears were filled with the sounds of whines, barks, and metal dog bowls scraping the concrete floor. I watched Todd, part man, part boy, move slowly up and down the aisles.

He seemed determined to give each animal a fair audition. After ten minutes, I decided to join him. Dog picking looked like fun. Besides that, I was vaguely curious about the dogs. The stiffness that was stubbornly rooted in my right leg was barely noticeable as I got up from the bench and walked along with Todd. He stopped at each cage and made mental notes that he occasionally shared with me.

"This one reminds me of Trudy. She is happy to see me." Trudy belonged to my son Jonathan and was Todd's favorite old dog. She was a Border collie with a tinge of German shepherd thrown into the mix. When she was a puppy, Jonathan would bring her out to the farm. She loved to help Todd move the sheep out of the back pasture and into the barnyard, where they were safe from the coyotes, bobcats, and foxes.

"Could be a sheep herder extraordinaire!" I said.

Todd moved slowly to the next cage to inspect a floppy-eared dog that wouldn't bother to amble over and greet us. She was liver-colored with white splotches on her chest and front legs, with the distinct black muzzle of a coonhound.

"She's quiet," Todd observed.

"Yep." I read out loud from the tag at the top of her cage. "The shelter named her Sally. This says she is an eight-year-old female coonhound and spaniel mix. Spayed. Can sit and roll over on command." I turned to Todd and said, "Hey, that dog takes orders better than some of my children."

Todd rolled his eyes at me. At this rate we would be here for a month, so I returned to the bench and the day-old newspaper that was about to become cage liner.

After wading through the sports and weather sections, I glanced up. Todd had progressed past only two more cages. He looked so much in his element. It occurred to me that if there were angels for animals, then surely Todd was one. I realized that some dog was going to be very lucky. Hayley worked her way back to check on Todd and seemed to like the way he studied each animal. She followed along and the two of them worked as a team in this most important selection. She didn't try to push him toward one of the less adoptable dogs. Instead, she tried to give explanations for every dog's condition.

As they stopped at each cage, Hayley encouraged Todd to get a closer look. My guess was that Hayley was spending more time with Todd than she did with the other visitors to the shelter.

"This is Baron. He appears to be a German short-haired pointer. He's lived in a cage most of his life. His owner thought that because he was a hunting dog, it would ruin him to run about the yard. He needs to be socialized. You know, spend more time around people. He could be a good pet, but he'll need a very patient and kind owner to teach him to trust humans again."

She opened the cage door. "He's scared," Todd said as he

wrapped his arms around the trembling dog. Almost immediately, the dog settled down and began to wag his tail, sensing that he was safe and in good hands.

Hayley looked at the tag on the door and said, "He's only been here four days. It takes some dogs longer than others to become comfortable. He seems to have taken to you right away. Dogs are good judges of character."

"Hayley, why do some of the dogs seem excited to see me and others don't?"

"That's a good question. Some dogs are still stuck on their old owners. They aren't ready yet to accept a new family or friend. Every dog in here has a perfect human match. There's not a dog in here that won't act excited when the right person comes along."

"How come those dogs are separated?" He pointed to an area separated from where they were by a chain-link fence with a gate and a sign that said DO NOT ENTER.

"They're in quarantine, not suitable for adoption."

"What's quarantine?" he asked.

"There are state laws about dogs that bite. They have to be isolated to make sure they do not have rabies."

Todd walked over to the fence and peered into the quarantine pens. "Why do those dogs all look the same?"

Hayley's expression darkened. "Most are pit bulls that the sheriff had to bring in because they have been mistreated. How a man treats a dog, Todd, says a lot about what's in his heart."

Before he could ask any more questions, Hayley led

Todd in a happier direction, toward a safer dog. "This big girl we call Pork Chop, because she is a little overweight." Pork Chop was a mixed-breed big black dog.

"Her owner came in to claim her last week, and when we told him there was a fifty-dollar boarding fee, he told us that he was going out to his truck to get a check. We waited for him, but he just drove off and never came back."

Todd stared at her in disbelief. "Why didn't he come and get his dog? She was waiting for him. Was there something wrong with that man?"

"I'd say so, Todd. I'd say something seriously wrong. Shame of it is that large black dogs, like Pork Chop, are the hardest to place with new owners. We call it the 'big black dog syndrome.'"

"Why's that?" Todd asked.

"Because there are so many of them; supply and demand."

Hayley reached the next cage and said, "Now, what is different about this dog?"

Todd stared and said, "He's little."

"That's right. Did you notice that he is the only little dog in the shelter?"

Todd looked around at the cages and asked, "Why is he the only one?"

"Well, we call them 'squat-and-pee' dogs.' They're house dogs. They are let out briefly, they squat, pee, and come back inside. Large dogs are left outside, often for hours. They break out of fences and end up here."

"What kind is he?" Todd asked.

"He's a Jack Russell mix."

"I like 'squat-and-pee dog' better!" I chimed in from my perch on the bench.

Todd frowned at my attempt at humor and then stopped in front of the only empty cage in the shelter and asked, "What happened to that one?"

Hayley smiled. "Probably out with a handler for a walk or grooming."

"Grooming?"

"We do lots of things, Todd, to help the animals be adopted. You might notice that we never allow their waste to stay in their cages. We've learned that people will walk right by a cage that has been fouled and that's not fair to the dog, is it?"

"No." Todd shook his head.

"We also have learned that people won't adopt a dog that is too scared. So we work a great deal with frightened dogs so that they welcome visitors. We all know that people pick dogs based on how they look. Polly, for instance, was here for thirty-nine days. Forty days is a very important date for these dogs. They really need to be adopted by then. When Polly was still here after thirty-five, we were worried. She was a very happy and friendly dog, so we called a lady here in town, a volunteer groomer. She came in and gave Polly a haircut, a shampoo, and bought her a brand-new collar with a pink ribbon on it. She did a great job. Yesterday was Polly's thirty-ninth day and . . ."—she grabbed Todd's arm excitedly—"someone adopted her this morning! So, Polly is at her new home."

I was hoping that Todd would not ask the significance of forty days and was pleased that Hayley did not come right out and say what happened to these dogs if they did not find a home for them. Todd would have been troubled by the ugly truth. The concept troubled me too. I got up from the bench again and quietly followed behind Todd and Hayley for another half hour of detailed dog inspections.

It was approaching the lunch hour before they had looked at all the dogs and Todd heard all their stories. I was surprised that he had not yet made his selection. I wasn't sure if he had not found the right dog or if he just wanted to take them all.

"Do you want to see one more?" Hayley asked.

She led us into an area at the very back of the shelter where a few empty cages sat. The only occupied cage held a large black lab retriever mix. Another "big black dog problem," it appeared.

Hayley offered her comments. "He's an older dog. You can tell by the gray around his muzzle. He's quiet, not a barker. We don't allow the dogs to be adopted for the first three days. This gives the owner a chance to claim their pet if it is just lost, but after the third day, the dog becomes the property of the shelter. Starting today, he's ours."

"What's his name?" I heard Todd ask as Hayley opened the cage door.

She looked around the door for information, but finding

none, she shrugged her shoulders. "Don't know, I guess he just showed up. They do that sometimes. He hasn't been here long enough for us to give him a name."

Todd seemed to hesitate. I had a good feeling about this dog. He sat, patiently aware, without jumping, barking, or whining, like many of the other dogs did when the cage door opened. He seemed focused, ready to receive a command, but his wagging tail showed that he was also pleased to see Todd.

Perhaps I was becoming a little bored by the selection process or I felt sorry for him because he was new to the shelter. I walked toward Todd and put my hand on his arm to get his attention. "Should we look him over?"

Todd didn't say no, so Hayley had him out of the cage in an instant. She gave the command "Sit," and he did so. The dog waited quietly while Todd ran his fingers through the gray and black hair on the nape of his neck. Then Todd stooped down so that he was at the dog's eye level and stared into his face for a few moments. He had warm green eyes that showed a certain patient wisdom.

After Todd sized him up, Hayley placed a choke chain around the dog's neck. He suddenly became excited, as if he knew he had been chosen. She snapped a leash on the collar and led him a few feet in one direction and then a few feet back the other way. He did not act like an animal that had spent much time in a cage. Hayley then issued several commands accompanied by a gesture. First, she held her palm outward, like a traffic cop directing a stop, and then she slowly bent her wrist so her fingertips pointed down toward the floor and again issued the command "Sit." The dog sat. Then she pushed the air down like she was cramming trash into a bag and said, "Down." The dog slid down onto his stomach. She said, "Stay," dropped the leash, and walked away. After she had taken ten steps, she turned to look back. He had not budged.

"He minds well, though he seems to have some age-related stiffness in his haunches."

Todd bent down, petted the dog, and ran his hands over his ribs. "He's thin. Is he eating?"

"He's eating. I bet he's been on the road for a while and missed a few meals."

Todd parted his fur and found a few rough spots, including a cut that had only recently scabbed over. He motioned to Hayley to look at the wound.

She kneeled down for a closer look. "We'll put something on it." She then looked approvingly at Todd. He had obviously noticed something important that even she had missed.

Todd stood up, folded his arms across his chest as if he were a discriminating and seasoned buyer of fine purebreds, and asked me, "What do you think, Dad?"

I walked around the dog twice, noticing four legs, a tail, and all the other required appendages. "He looks excellent to me," I offered.

Todd grinned happily and pointed confidently at the animal. "We'll take him." Finally, the dog jumped up from his resting spot, as if on command, and edged toward the exit. Hayley grabbed the leash and held him in place.

I did not waste any time in confirming the terms of our arrangement. "When do we bring him back, Todd?"

"We bring him back on the twenty-sixth, Dad. That's when Christmas ends." I looked to Hayley for reassurance and she smiled and shook her head approvingly.

Todd and Mary Ann had gone into town a few days earlier and had used some of Todd's allowance money to purchase a leash and collar. Given the time of the year, Mary Ann suggested a green collar and a red leash. They had selected a medium-sized collar, which Todd pulled out of his coat pocket and easily slipped around the dog's neck. Hayley shut the cage door behind us and Todd led the dog back into the reception area on the festive-looking red leash.

Passing all the other dogs on the way out, I felt a little sorry that they were not adopted for Christmas too. There was a fleeting moment when I considered taking two, but my reputation had to be considered, so I moved on. We filled out some paperwork and Hayley put some ointment on the cut.

After thanking her, we left the shelter with our new friend. The crisp winter wind caught my breath, but I managed to ask, "Do you want to name him?"

"Already did," Todd said to my surprise as he hurried toward the truck.

"What?"

"I named him *'Christmas.'*" Todd opened the truck door

and Christmas instantly jumped in. Todd climbed in next to the dog and I got in behind the wheel, oddly at ease with this warm furry presence comfortably wedged between my son and me. As I started the ignition, the radio came to life, a Christmas song filling the cold Kansas air.

I looked at Todd and the dog and said, "That's a good name. That's a real good name."

CHAPTER 4

In the truck on the way home, the dog was well behaved. I suspected that it was not his first ride in a pickup truck. But for the occasional wag of his tail, he did not fidget or move around, nor whine or growl. Todd massaged the dog's muscles and ran his hands through his coat. This must have felt good, for Christmas turned around several times and gave Todd an approving lick. I couldn't resist reaching over and patting him a few times myself. He seemed very content with us.

"Where do you think we should keep Christmas this week?" I asked Todd.

Todd looked at me, surprised. "In my room."

"I was thinking maybe we should put him in the chicken coop to guard the hens. How about that?"

"Nah, Dad, chickens don't need a guard."

"Well, how about at the bottom of the silo? I have seen some rats down there and I bet he could keep 'em out of there."

"Nah, Dad, I think my room works."

"You did clean it up, didn't you, Todd?"

"Six sacks. I took out six sacks."

"That'll make enough room for him, won't it? Now, you're sure you don't want that elephant?"

Todd laughed at the idea. "Nope. I like Christmas."

As we passed back through Crossing Trails, I noticed a trickle of Christmas shoppers exiting various stores with wrapped presents or shopping bags in hand. There was a movement by the local chamber of commerce to keep shoppers in town, but I wondered if their campaign was working. Once on the highway, making our way back to the farm, it occurred to me that there had been many times when I just did not know what to get Todd for Christmas. As he sat beside me with that dog, I knew that this year was different.

When we arrived home, Mary Ann met us at the back door. "What took so long? I was beginning to worry about you two."

"Dog picking is hard work. It takes time." Mary Ann knew that Todd could be very deliberate on matters that were important to him, so she dropped the subject as the three of us came in out of the cold, through the back porch door and into the kitchen.

Todd led the dog around in circles. Christmas appeared

to be just as well trained and obedient for us as he was for Hayley. He heeled appropriately, and when Todd stopped, he promptly sat down beside him and waited for the next cue. Todd had apparently paid close attention to Hayley and repeated the same series of commands for his mother's benefit.

Mary Ann carried on like she had just witnessed the construction of the Eighth Wonder of the World. "George, look how the dog minds. Look how Todd can work with him. Isn't it amazing!"

"Incredible," I muttered.

Mary Ann leaned over so that she could look directly into Christmas's face and exclaimed, "He has green eyes. I love dogs with green eyes."

"He was the best one at the shelter," Todd said, giving Christmas a pat and removing the leash. The dog's tail thumped the floor as he wagged it, a sound that would become familiar in the coming week.

"Todd, that dog could not have been at the shelter. He is perfect."

"Mom, can I tell you about the shelter?"

"Why, of course, sweetie. Tell me all about it."

Todd was as animated as I had seen him in years. He grabbed his mother's hand and led her, the dog right behind them, to the kitchen table, where the two of them sat, with Christmas at their feet. Todd told his mother all about the shelter. He described virtually every dog, while Mary Ann patiently listened. I leaned against the wall and just observed, experiencing the whole trip again, this time through Todd's eyes.

While they talked, I opened doors and rummaged through kitchen cabinets until I found two old steel bowls shoved in the very back as if waiting for me to unearth them all these years later: Tucker's old dog dishes. Somehow I felt comfort and not sadness.

I ran some water from the tap into one bowl and put it under the table for Christmas. I put some of the dog food that Todd and Mary Ann had purchased in the other bowl and set it next to the water. Christmas, not wanting to be rude, gently removed a few morsels from the bowl and quietly nibbled away while Todd and Mary Ann gossiped about his canine cousins at the shelter.

In our hall closet I found an old blanket on a shelf and I placed it on the kitchen floor. Christmas approached and pawed until all was situated properly, as dogs will do. Once it was acceptable, he lay down on his new bed. Leaning against the door frame, I listened to Todd recount the remainder of the day's adventure to his mother. They were so absorbed in conversation that I don't think they'd noticed me playing innkeeper.

Fifteen minutes passed with only an occasional pause for breath. I finally interrupted. "I offered to get him an elephant, but he passed."

"Oh, George, let him tell his story."

After all the events had been thoroughly reported, Todd and Mary Ann gave Christmas a tour of our small home.

Apparently this approval process worked both ways and they wanted to be sure that Christmas found our accommodations to his liking. They moved out of the kitchen into Todd's room and the guest room, through the dining room, and finally to the living room, which stretched across the entire front of our home. Against the interior wall of the living room is a fireplace that warms our house.

Todd, dragging the dog's blanket along, stopped within range of the radiant heat cast from the fire. He spread the blanket out, marking their territory, and sat down on the floor. Christmas stretched out and ordered up a canine massage that Todd gladly administered, starting with his paws and finishing with just the right amount of therapeutic belly rubbing. Christmas yawned and Todd lay down beside him for a lazy rest by the fire. It seemed that our weary traveler had found a comfortable place and a good friend.

When Christmas woke from his afternoon snooze, he made his way through the kitchen to the back door and let out one small bark as if he had done it a million times. Mary Ann let him out and we were all pleased that Christmas was not shy about communicating his needs to us—one less worry about having a dog in the house.

By the next morning, a warm front had moved in and the snow was melting fast beneath a blue sky crowded with large scattered clouds. Several geese were honking loudly as they made their way from our lake and into our fields for a day of foraging for the bits of sorghum, corn, and oats that the combine generously left behind.

Todd and Christmas were still asleep while Mary Ann and I ate breakfast. My experience with sleepovers told me that last night might have been more about talking than sleeping. I left Mary Ann humming at the kitchen sink when I left to do my chores.

After feeding the stock, I turned and saw the two of them, Todd and Christmas, ambling toward me.

"Good morning," Todd said.

"How's that dog?"

"He's fine." Todd slipped through the rails of the corral and started to inspect the cattle. Christmas started to follow him in. Not wanting him to spook the herd, I said, "Christmas, sit." I used the same hand signal that Hayley used and he went straight to his haunches.

Todd grinned at me in his lopsided way. "Good dog picker, aren't I?"

"Indeed, you are a fine dog picker." I went over and scratched the dog's head and his tail wagged excitedly. I softly praised him, "Good boy, Christmas." After Todd left the corral, I said, "Okay, Christmas, good boy, you can go now."

He spun a few circles and stood by Todd. "Can I go to the creek with the dog?"

"Sure."

"Can I drive the truck down?"

It was a treat for Todd to drive the truck, even though his mother insisted that he keep the transmission in first gear. I fished my car keys out of my pocket and handed them over. "You just drive slowly or your mom will have me sleeping in the barn."

Todd opened the truck door. Christmas hopped in and once again settled easily on the middle of the bench seat. Todd started the engine and headed ever so slowly south toward Kill Creek. The creek always fascinated him.

For some reason, as I watched them leave, it occurred to me that I was about Todd's age when Tucker died. How different Todd's early adult life was from mine.

These thoughts made me grateful that I wasn't saying good-bye to my son as he boarded a military bus, bidding this dog a final farewell. Todd would never have to know that returning home was only the first part of a difficult journey back. My Vietnam memories remain painful, but I've grown better at working my way through the resentment.

It's important to have a few choice spots for sitting and thinking, places that resonate with good memories and ample privacy. The whole idea of watching a son you love go off to war sent me straight to my favorite sitting spot at the back of the barn, furnished with a three-legged milking stool that my great-grandfather hewed from an oak tree right here on this farm.

Considering the unpleasant memories of war service was something that the army psychologist encouraged us to do. Even after all these years, with very little effort, I can still close my eyes and hear bomb blasts, the rapid fire of the M-16s, the heavy thuds of a .45-caliber pistol, the shouts, the pleas, the orders, choppers, F-4s dropping napalm, and against it all—insects, a dull roar of crickets, gnats, mosquitoes, and flies.

In the middle of winter, I could imagine the oppressive damp jungle heat. After enough remembering, I opened my eyes and tried to think of happier memories from that time in my life.

Mary Ann wrote me every day. Her letters are in a box on the top shelf of my closet. I tried to break up with her before leaving. I told her that she was too young to be sitting around waiting for me to come back, if I ever did. Because she was two years older than me, I kidded her that she had better act fast before her marrying years were a faded memory.

She would have none of it. After all the teasing about robbing the cradle, she was not giving up on me. When it was time for us to break up, she would let me know. Mary Ann said she would be there for me then and always.

We were married six months after I got back and she has been true to her word ever since.

My leg was stiff, so I got up to take a look at Tucker's old dog collar that hung on the wall. Turning to go inside for lunch, I heard the Ford truck grinding slowly toward the house in first gear. I felt better, grateful to be right there on the farm with my son. I was so pleased that Todd was not a young man going off to war. Little did I know that day how close I was to finally completing my journey home.

The barn door flew open. Todd was shouting, "Dad,

guess what Christmas and I found! Cat tracks at the creek that were as big as my hands!" He held his big paws up in the air.

"Those would be very big prints. I don't think bobcats are that big and there hasn't been a cougar around here in years."

"They sure looked like big cat prints to me, Dad."

I thought a minute. "When the snow melts, it plays tricks on you and it makes prints seem two or three times larger than their actual size." I laughed. "Did you see any giant raccoons down there?"

Todd thought about it. "No giant raccoons. I guess you're right. It was just a bobcat."

"Makes sense to me."

Many years ago, my grandfather told me that when he was a young man out hunting, he heard that strange grunting noise deer make when they are startled. He turned and saw a cougar chase a doe into the forest. Just a few years back, another man I know, a lawyer in town, claimed to have seen a big cat flash across the eighth hole of the local golf course just as the sun was setting.

I put little confidence in these sightings for several reasons. Sooner or later most wild animals in these parts end up tangling with a car and losing. I had never seen or heard of that happening to a cougar in our area. Also, bobcats are much bigger than people think and they move so quickly that they could easily be mistaken for a larger cat.

Still there was one thing that made me wonder. It had

been four years ago and I couldn't explain it then, so I forgot about it until now. A cow and a newborn calf got out through our fence. Two miles south of us are nearly a thousand acres of privately owned timber, left untouched for generations, if not centuries. I rode my mare, following the cattle tracks deep into the timber, until I came to a small creek.

The creek bed was damp and there were occasional pools of water collecting gnats and mosquitoes. There was not much of a trail and I had to constantly push spiderwebs out of my face to make progress. The cow and calf had stopped to drink. Given the volume of tracks, they had lingered there for several hours, perhaps all night. Cows have cloven hooves and leave distinct prints. I saw strange tracks around the edge of the pool. I got down off the horse for a closer look. There appeared to be cat prints the size of my hand stamped in the mud.

Not wanting to add my name to the list of local crackpots who swore to mountain lion sightings, I never said a thing. Later that morning, I found the missing cow and calf unharmed and forgot about the whole incident.

There was little risk in being careful, so I cautioned Todd as he walked away, "Just the same, maybe you and Christmas should stay away from the creek for a few days. I'll check on those tracks later."

Todd shrugged his shoulders. "Sure, Dad, but that cougar is no match for Christmas."

"You're wrong there. No dog can take a cougar."

Todd and Christmas left the barn and I walked slowly up to the house behind them. Christmas circled back several times, apparently wondering why I was so slow. When Todd wasn't looking, I crouched down and he kissed my face and wagged his tail. Todd was a fine dog picker.

On the days leading up to the holiday, I tried to put the war and memories of Tucker and Good Charlie aside, but it wasn't easy. Several times Mary Ann would stop and ask me, "Are you all right?"

"Yes," I told her, but she knew when I was struggling with those memories.

"Is it the dog?"

"No," I answered, though we both knew I was lying.

CHAPTER 5

On Saturday, the day before our holiday open house, the temperatures were still moderate but the wind speed had increased. Because the breeze was blowing from the south, we would continue to enjoy warmer than normal weather. After Todd, Christmas, and I finished the morning chores, I drove the tractor down to the back field to check on the mystery tracks Todd had seen a few days earlier.

As I headed south toward Kill Creek, the wind blew even harder and I had to pull my jacket tightly around me and put on my gloves. Most of the snow had melted off the ground and the fields were wet but not yet muddy. Some green shoots of grass sporadically peeked up, but most of the fields had put on winter browns, tans, and grays.

I did not hurry the tractor along and instead enjoyed the time outdoors to think.

On the television that morning the political pundits were jawing about the latest war and I started to wonder why I could never make sense out of these debates. Behind me I pulled an old yellow and green John Deere manure spreader that cast cattle waste into the meadow—nature's fertilizer—and it occurred to me that these talking heads were spouting the same stuff I was spreading. They debated war like it could be right or wrong and like they were somehow uniquely positioned to know the difference. On the microscopic level of one soldier, I knew that wars seldom make sense, and maybe that's why I struggled listening to their dialogues.

Slowing the tractor down, I crossed over a culvert and then passed through a wooded hedgerow where I had to protect my head from low-hanging branches. A pair of red foxes sauntered out of the woods and through the meadow. I pushed in the clutch of the tractor and watched. Like most foxes, they were unbothered by a mere human. After they passed out of sight, sliding the throttle down a notch, I let out the clutch and continued toward the creek, my mind returning to the war debates.

There was another tragedy of war that was never discussed or even acknowledged and this one had bothered me a great deal over the years. Thousands of dogs served in Vietnam and saved countless lives, including my own. No awards or medals were ever given to these brave and loyal dogs. It was as if it did not matter when a dog sacrificed his life.

Few of these war dogs survived and the ones that did

were callously abandoned. It had to be traumatizing for the remaining soldiers to evacuate and leave behind a friend that would lay down his life, not just once but every day. Each time I thought about it, I became hurt and angry.

The creek was in sight and I saw an owl fly just over the treetops and land in a giant sycamore that stood at one side of the creek crossing. I stopped the tractor just short of the creek and sat. I could smell the distant odor of a wood fire, perhaps my own. This area of our farm never stopped being beautiful to me. It was a good place for putting life into perspective. I could hear the water moving gently through the riverbed, not like a roaring Colorado mountain stream teeming with trout and gold dust but like a river that takes its time and can say a lot if you have the patience to listen, which is exactly what I did. My mood lifted thanks to its wise counsel.

I turned the tractor off and applied the emergency brake, climbed down, and then looked for tracks. There were plenty of them. Raccoons, birds, rabbits, size 12 Converse tennis shoes, and a Christmas dog, but I did not see any big cat prints. So, I got back on the tractor and headed home, with the transmission in low gear.

Twice later that day, when Todd left Christmas alone for a few minutes, the dog wandered down to the barnyard and found me. He came over and nudged me, sliding his head under my hand, as if to say, "Pet me."

Wanting to see if he would follow commands for me like he had done for Hayley, I used this time to practice—sit, stay, and roll over—with him. I even got him to fetch and bring me an old tennis ball on command. He was very obedient and I had the sense that this dog, just like Good Charlie or Tucker, would give everything asked of him. Kneeling down, I held Christmas's face close to mine and felt his warm breath and soft ears. "You're a keeper," I said, without realizing the irony of my words.

I liked the smell of this animal. All of the outdoor scents that I recognized from our farm seemed to waltz freely through his fur, distilled and mixed into a nice natural aroma that was the outdoors I loved.

Remembering and missing my other old canine friends, I hugged Christmas extra hard. He seemed to understand. He rested his muzzle on my shoulder and pressed his cold nose against my ear as if to say he was very happy to be with us. When I released him, Christmas ambled over and picked up his ball and dropped it by my feet.

"You're pretty direct, aren't you?" I tossed the ball as far as I could and he chased after it. Good Charlie liked to play fetch too, although he preferred a Frisbee.

We buried Good Charlie in a graveyard by a small Buddhist monastery in the foothills near our base at Tan Son Nhut. When we told his story to the monks, they conferred among themselves for a few minutes and then concluded that Good Charlie was a reincarnated American war hero from our distant history. They seemed very pleased to have his presence with them and they promised to care for his grave. They undoubtedly meant it.

I have a couple of tangible reminders from those days of my life. One is a scar than runs from my buttocks down to my right knee like an ugly set of pink railroad tracks. The second is a damaged right leg, which, while keeping me on military disability pay, still throbs, aches, and causes me to move slower than I would like. Last, there is a purple heart in the top drawer of the dresser by my bed. Someday I plan on hanging that medal where it belongs—on Good Charlie's grave.

Christmas whined for me to attend to the ball he dropped at my feet and forced me away from my thoughts. I looked at him and said, "Well, old boy, taking you back may not be as easy as I thought, but a deal is a deal. Right?"

Christmas was sitting down and I took a wild guess and said, "Shake, boy, shake." Sure enough he held out his paw and we shook on it.

It was nice to have a dog around again and I remembered how special the friendship between members of the human and canine worlds can be. I tossed the ball toward the house and we both headed in for supper.

Mary Ann decided to make the evening meal an event. She set the table in the dining room with special Christmas dishes that our daughter had given us some years back. The table was covered with one of her favorite Christmas tablecloths, and red and green candles were arranged as a centerpiece.

After dinner, we helped Mary Ann clean up the dishes, a chore that Christmas cheerfully performed, licking up every last scrap of food. We spent the rest of the evening watching television in the living room warmed by the fire. Eventually, I shut off the lights and we headed up the old stairs for bed.

When the sun leaves the winter sky, temperatures drop quickly. Even with the addition of insulation and central heat in the 1970s, our old house is still often cold, making pajamas and electric blankets necessary winter companions. That night, after I was in bed under the warm covers, Mary Ann felt especially good beside me. We could hear Todd muttering something to Christmas in his room downstairs.

"I think he likes that dog, George."

"You sure about that?" I asked.

"How about you, George—do you like the dog?"

"Oh, yeah, I suppose so. If you like the furry types, he'll do."

"You seemed better today."

"I felt better, much better."

"What was wrong, George?" she asked as she held my forearm.

"I had some thinking to do."

"You expected this, didn't you?" she asked.

"Yes, I suppose so." She rested her head on my shoulder and I said, "I want to thank you for something."

"What's that?"

"Have I told you enough just how much all of your letters meant to me?"

"You've told me a thousand times."

"I should have told you a million times. Thanks again, Mary Ann."

"I love you, George."

"I love you too. Good night."

CHAPTER 6

S unday, December 20, arrived and we readied for our
family dinner and neighborhood open house. The
scent of roasting ham and turkey wove its way down to the
barnyard, making the swine and fowl nervous. Steam from
the mashed potatoes condensed on the kitchen windows
and coffee percolated in the old pot on the stove top. Several
times during the day, I interrupted my work to inspect Mary
Ann's efforts, using the taste method. My timing was good.
Around two o'clock, I came in just as Mary Ann pulled
sugar cookies in the shape of Christmas trees out of the
oven. Oatmeal cookies were already cooling on the old oak
countertop. Todd, Christmas, and I decided it was too much
for Mary Ann to do all on her own.

We stacked the cookies we didn't eat on Christmas
plates, set the table, and made last-minute adjustments to

the lights and other decorations. Todd and I took showers and then the three males (two human and one canine) fell asleep for a brief winter's nap beneath an old quilt by the fire that crackled with the scent of pine and cedar logs. The rest of the afternoon, Todd and I did little more than add logs to the fire, make dog observations, and listen to the sound of rain falling hard and fast on the rooftop.

My children and their families began coming through the back door in the early evening hours. Only strangers ever came to the front door. The rain let up, but a gentle winter drizzle still fell. The melting snow and the newly fallen rain moved through a thousand little ditches, gullies, and rivulets. From the back porch, as I greeted my family, I could hear the water in Kill Creek rushing rapidly toward its confluence with the Kaw River.

As my children and grandchildren made their way in, quick hugs and kisses were exchanged and the house came alive with the sounds of holiday greetings. Coats, hats, and scarves were discarded as Todd pulled all family members to the front of the house to meet our honored guest, Christmas, basking by the heat of the fire.

This dog wasn't much into formal introductions and he stayed on his blanket, though he allowed head patting and scratching behind the ears. His wide bushy tail swept across the floor in a measured way that showed he sincerely enjoyed making each and every new acquaintance. After everyone arrived, we sat down to eat and to catch up on the latest family gossip.

At dinner, Todd again explained the Adopt a Dog for Christmas program to his extended family. Christmas rolled over onto his stomach and rested his head on his front paws. His ears perked up and he listened, as if he sensed he was the topic of conversation.

My daughter, Hannah, and my daughters-in-law all thought it was about the sweetest thing they had ever heard. My sons just grinned and I suspected that they were thinking, *Dad sure got suckered on this one.*

As we passed plate after plate of food, each member of my family tossed glances in the dog's direction and offered some kind words of reassurance to Todd. "I'm sure he is the best dog at the shelter, maybe in the whole county." "You're sure a handsome old boy" was mixed in with a lot of "You're a good boy. Yes, you are."

Todd and I just smiled. We were, after all, very good dog pickers.

Christmas seemed to relish the praise, and with every passing compliment he inched his way off the blanket and scooted ever closer to the table. Eventually, he just got up and joined us, perched, as any dog with the least amount of intelligence would be, directly beneath the dining room table and within easy reach of socked feet that brushed across his fur and hands that "accidentally" dropped bits of tasty dinner.

There was one aspect of the Adopt a Dog for Christmas program that had been overlooked in our explanation and I wanted to clear it up. In a matter-of-fact way, I asked, "Now, don't forget, Todd, when does Christmas end?"

Todd looked down at his plate and repeated, "Christmas ends on the twenty-sixth. That's when he has to go home to the shelter."

I should have known better. This was the wrong time to bring it up and the idea of returning Christmas to the shelter put a chill in the air. There were scowls on the prettier faces at the table. My sons were looking at me in disbelief, even disapproval. Anxiety was welling up in my chest again. The awkward silence that lingered in the air told me that I had a problem on my hands.

I was trying to do something nice for Todd and this dog, and now if I didn't keep him, it would be me and not Christmas who would be crated and sent back to the shelter. I didn't know what to do.

Sitting there silently, I allowed the others to carry on the conversation, which seemed inevitably to make its way back to Christmas. Suddenly I felt as if I were on the outside looking in.

Our canine guest ambled around the dinner table for pats on the head, kind words, scraps of meat, and other delicacies. I just rolled my eyes. There didn't seem to be any effort to teach him table manners. Every woman at the table took her respective turn at adoration. My daughter, Hannah, a recently divorced accountant with no children of her own, started it. She held Christmas's head in her hands and began talking in a way that made me sink even lower in my chair, with my arms folded across my chest.

"Christmas, I do believe you are the most handsome and

kind dog I have ever known." Christmas accepted praise in a very dignified manner, as if he had much experience with adoration. Hannah continued, "Why in the world would anyone put you in a shelter?" She looked up to me and asked again, incredulously, "Why was he in the shelter?"

"No one knows for sure. They said he just showed up." I tried to change the subject away from the dog. "Say, Hannah, I have a question on my taxes this year."

"Dad, I bet the Adopt a Dog for Christmas expenses are deductible. Do you think anybody has checked to make sure he has had all of his shots? Maybe you should do that for him. I bet the vet would come out tomorrow if you called now."

Then the boys took their turn talking to the dog. They were having a great deal of fun and I was sure it was at my expense. My oldest son, Jonathan, a finish carpenter married to his high school sweetheart, had three boys of his own. Being the oldest, he undoubtedly felt it was his duty to make sure the boys were not outdone by their sister.

"Well, old boy, this could be your last Christmas in front of a warm fire. Who knows where you'll be next year? Why don't you just take this turkey and go eat it. I've got lots of turkey dinners left in *my* life." Jonathan handed Christmas a large cut of dark meat and the dog ambled back to the fireplace.

I wondered if the dog would be ordering up room service anytime soon. They were all having a great deal of fun, but I was not laughing.

Thomas, the youngest of my three older boys, speculated

with a wide grin and intermittent bursts of laughter that at Christmas's age any change of environment could be stressful. "Dad, be careful moving the poor dog back to the animal shelter. It's not that comfortable in the back of your old truck. Maybe you could put a mattress in the truck bed for him."

Ryan, the middle of these three older boys, was blessed with a quiet nature. He felt the need to emphasize each of his siblings' observations only with a wide grin. His eyes twinkled in amusement and I just kept squirming in my chair.

Maybe it was my imagination, but it seemed that each time the subject of Christmas came up, every man, woman, and child looked at me. Todd, of course, understood none of the subtleties of the conversation, but was generally pleased that his dog was commanding so much attention.

About the time the bigger eaters were going into the kitchen for seconds, Todd excused himself from the table, leaving half a plate of food unfinished. Christmas followed him to the edge of the dining room. "Look, everybody," Todd said. With Christmas by his side, he began to issue orders. "Sit!" The dog sat. Todd continued with the commands for shake, lie down, and stay. In each case, Christmas gladly complied. When he said "Stay" and walked toward the fireplace, the audience could stand it no more and broke into a raucous applause. Todd then allowed Christmas to come and sit beside him and feel the warmth of the fire.

After the two of them were comfortably situated, Todd turned on his radio, put on his headphones, and began singing his own versions of Christmas songs, loud and off-key.

Christmas tilted his head back and started to howl. Thankfully, we were in the privacy of our home, because the laughter was uncontrolled as Todd's older siblings had to restrain themselves from falling out of their chairs.

After the laughter died down, Mary Ann changed the mood by mounting her first open assault on my scantily fortified position. She said, in a voice I knew to be short on negotiation, "I can't remember when Todd has found something he has enjoyed more than taking care of this dog. He has been very responsible and those two have a special bond."

I foolishly dug in my heels. "Yes," I said. "And when does Christmas end?"

There was a long pause. Mary Ann folded her napkin and rather resolutely placed it back on the table, as if to signal that she was upping the ante. I had the distinct feeling that my wartime ally was about to abandon me. "George, I've heard the reverend say that we should act with generosity and kindness every day and not just on Christmas!" She picked up her napkin and wiped her mouth firmly to remove any unkind words or thoughts that might reside on her lips. The uncomfortable feeling in my chest was growing worse.

Considering a response, but knowing none would work,

I just hung my head and finished my dinner in silence. Perhaps I was beaten and there was no use in fighting it any longer. I was prepared to keep Christmas. In fact, I would have liked it. My fears of owning another dog seemed misplaced and I was enjoying his company. But there was another reason why Christmas needed to return to the shelter. Perhaps the most important reason was that my son and I made a deal and I wanted him to stick to it. I wanted Todd to learn to be more like an adult and less like a child. Adults keep their promises, even when they become inconvenient. Adults have to learn that things can be good without being forever.

Everybody seemed to be missing another important point. For the Adopt a Dog for Christmas program to work, families should not feel pressured to keep the animals. If I kept Christmas this year, I would not be back to the shelter next year or any other year.

With dinner behind us, we cleaned off the table, washed the dishes, and began answering the knocks on the back door as the parade of old friends, family, and neighbors made their annual visit with candy, cookies, pies, cakes, and small wrapped presents.

My grandfather's duties as county road maintainer had ended decades ago, so these visits were rooted in tradition alone. The wives seemed to lead this parade and behind them followed their husbands with their hands in their pockets. This was a Christmas ritual that I could have done without this year.

It wasn't the train under the tree or the doll in the cradle that brought them to the front room. It was Todd tugging on their shirtsleeves and insisting that they visit Christmas.

Jonathan showed no mercy for my condition and led the rural masses to the throne. "I want you to see something really special, Hank. This is Christmas, *Todd's* dog." He looked up at me and grinned.

Hank was an eighty-eight-year-old dairy farmer and someone whom I often looked up to as the father I had lost. He was sharp, fit, and worth a lot of money. His family farm was one of the oldest and most successful in this part of Kansas. Hank inherited a strong work ethic and a proud, determined outlook on life. A shrewd businessman, he had no time for an animal that did not turn a profit. Hank carried a soft spot for Todd and always took the time to show some interest in his life. It did not surprise me in the least that he too would make a big fuss over Christmas. Hank slowly bent over and scratched the dog's belly with his long wrinkled fingers as Todd explained for the umpteenth time the details of the shelter's program.

Hank patiently waited for Todd to finish. He removed the unlit cigar that was ever present in the corner of his mouth and then said, with the authority and wisdom that only age can bestow, "This is one fine animal." All the heads in the room nodded in agreement. Todd smiled.

Hank must have noticed that I was not joining in and said, "Why, what is wrong, George? Don't you like Christmas?"

Todd, bless his heart, came to my rescue. "No, Hank,

Dad likes Christmas. Dad helped me get Christmas. He helped me pick him out from all those dogs needing a place to go for the holidays."

Something that Todd said turned over in my head until it stuck. I rubbed my chin and the idea hit me square between the eyes. Hallelujah, salvation had come. I changed my perspective and stopped seeing myself as the villain. Todd was right; this was my program as much as it was his. I just needed to get with it.

Walking over to Christmas, I commented, "One of the best dogs I've ever seen, Hank. He is a dandy. Shame of it is . . . he isn't ours. Like Todd said, the county shelter loans them out over the holidays." I paused a moment and added, "You know, Hank, I've got the phone number in the kitchen. They're open till noon Christmas Eve; I bet you could adopt a dog for Christmas too!"

Hank acted as if he had touched a hot stove. He sprang to his feet, quickly backed away from Christmas, grabbed his wife's arm, and all but shouted, "No! You know we're way too old for dogs. Jean, we have other stops to make. We had best be moving."

"It's no bother, Hank. It will just take me a minute to grab the number." I started to leave the room when I looked over at Hank's wife and Mary Ann.

Mary Ann's countenance was angelic. She looked upon me with eyes that welled with tears. Her voice quivered as she said, "George, this is just the most wonderful thing you are doing for these dogs."

Jean pulled away from her husband of sixty-four years and walked toward me, beaming. "Of course, George, we would love to adopt a pet too. This is a terrific program that you and Todd are supporting."

She turned to Hank, who had become agitated and stiff. His tired face suddenly showed every bit of its eighty-eight years. "Well, honey, I think this is a wonderful idea too, but at our age?" He grabbed Jean's arm as if to plead his case. Jean peeled Hank off and froze him solid with a glare. Defeated, he looked down and muttered, "Yes, Jean, let's get the number. I suppose a dog for the holidays might make things merrier."

I put my arm around Hank and offered a consoling pat to the back. "You know, Hank, I bet that boy of mine would help you pick one out."

I looked around the room for Todd, but he wasn't anywhere to be seen. Each of his brothers seemed to be smirking. They knew exactly what I had done to poor old Hank Fisher and they relished his misery. I did not like it. The boys were having far too much fun at the expense of my old friend. It occurred to me how to make a good idea even better.

"Hank," I said, "if every one of us in this room adopted a dog—or at least made a call or two to our friends—I bet we could clean out the shelter for Christmas. What do you think?"

Hank shifted his weight from one foot to the other and did not see where I was going.

"It's kind of like foster care for dogs. You give them a nice place to stay for a week or so, longer if you want, and that's a good thing for the dog, but some of the people will end up keeping the pets. Maybe not you or me. In fact, Todd and I have agreed that our dog will go back on the twenty-sixth. But many people will keep their dogs. That's why the program works. Just think how many fine foster homes could come from this house alone!"

The implication of my proposal slowly sunk in. Hank smiled. "You mean, George, not just you and me adopt a dog for Christmas, but every family should. Jonathan, Hannah, Ryan, Thomas, all of them."

My older sons all stared at me in disbelief.

"That's right!" I said.

The bait was set. There was not one but three hard strikes as my lovely daughters-in-law buzzed about the room proclaiming, "What a wonderful idea. Can we have the phone number too?"

Soon everyone was making arrangements for their very own Christmas dog. In the background a cacophony of grandchildren's voices pleaded, "Yes, Daddy. Please, Daddy. Can we, Dad?" They buzzed about me for advice and information on dog picking, all of which I generously dispensed.

Not wanting to leave a skimpy margin for victory, I scanned the room again and found the son who had offered the least mercy toward his poor father. "Jonathan, with three boys of your own, perhaps you should consider three dogs."

Hank immediately understood the magnitude of my catch. His eyes glimmered with mischief as he looked slowly down at the carpet and added in a most serious tone, "It's a bad thing for a boy to feel left out, particularly it being Christmas and all."

I must admit that at times it is hard for me to leave well enough alone, and this was one of those moments. "Jonathan, if you like," I asked in the most humble and sincere voice I could muster, "I could send the vet down the road to your place to make sure your three are up on their shots too."

By ten o'clock things were slowing down. We had pitched the Adopt a Dog for Christmas program to all the visitors at our holiday open house that night, suggesting that it be part of the holiday tradition in Cherokee County for families to take a dog in for a week and show it a little kindness. Todd was very supportive and never once showed the least hesitation when I explained that our dog too was just a guest.

I tried to imagine the conversations my older boys were having in their cars on the way home that night, certain that my grandchildren were carrying on incessantly about their Christmas dogs. While a small pang of guilt came over me, it inspired me the way the children shifted their focus so easily from what gifts they hoped to receive to what dog they could help.

They would probably discuss breeds, age, and temperament, and then everyone would agree that there was no finer dog at the shelter than Christmas. They would just do their best to choose a dog. For, after all, each animal deserved a home for the holidays. I could also hear each of my sons asking, "And when does Christmas end?"

What Todd had begun was turning out well. Getting the children and grandchildren to focus on something besides themselves seemed to make them happier and Christmas more meaningful for us all.

Todd had fallen asleep on the couch. Mary Ann was carrying the last tumblers of half-consumed soda to the kitchen. His stomach full, Christmas seemed settled in for the night. His back was to the fire and his four legs stretched out into the room. While I would have normally let the fire die out, I threw on two more logs and closed the protective fire screen. I patted Christmas on the head and bent down to address the vehicle of my newly bestowed sainthood. "Well, old boy, we had quite a day, didn't we? Do you have any idea what you and Todd started?"

Christmas tilted his head and opened his sleepy green eyes. He looked at me and I'll be darned if his black lips didn't curl back into a smile. His tail lazily began to sweep to and fro. I had to admit, he was a good old dog. "Well, good night, Christmas, we'll see you in the morning." I put a blanket over Todd and turned off the light.

"Mary Ann," I called out softly, "I'm going to bed."

"I'll be up in a few minutes, George," I heard her say as I headed up the stairs. She said my name pleasantly, with all of the love she held for me in full flower.

I brushed my teeth, hung my jeans on their hook, put my boots under the bed, turned out the light, got under the covers, and waited for Mary Ann. As I was just drifting off to sleep, I heard the steps. They came quicker than I expected and with a spryness that I thought was lost. My surprise did not stop there.

She leaped onto the bed. When I reached out to touch her in the darkness, I felt warm fur in my hands. It was Christmas. "What in the world are you doing up here, old boy?" His tail thumped rhythmically and he felt warm against my legs. Slipping back down into bed, I decided not to make him move. What did it matter if he rested there for the night? I would be true to the program and be the best dog host possible, even if it was for only a short period of time.

I had fallen asleep by the time Mary Ann came to bed. She nudged me awake.

"George?" she asked.

Coming out of my not-too-deep sleep, I leaned up on my elbow. "Yes, what is it, dear?"

"I'm worried about you."

"Why is that?" I asked.

"You seem to have made a friend here."

"So?"

"George, when does Christmas end?"

"On the twenty-sixth, of course. Why do you ask?"

She pulled the covers around her shoulders, giggled softly to herself, and rolled over to sleep.

CHAPTER 7

The next morning, after I came in from doing my chores, I saw Todd on the phone in the kitchen as Mary Ann looked on.

"How many are left, Hayley?" he asked. Todd struggled with a pencil, numbering each line on a piece of paper from one through sixteen. "Wait a minute, I'm writing it down."

Todd slowly called the numbers out as he went. "Twelve, thirteen." Hayley Donaldson waited on him with great patience. Todd was now painstakingly writing a description of a dog on each line. I looked over his shoulder as he wrote in his crooked scrawl on the first line, "Huskee, Shiperd Mix, six, geerl."

My expression reflected exasperation with Todd's spelling, but Mary Ann frowned and placed her finger over her lips as she shushed me.

Christmas, the apparent crew chief of this operation, was at Todd's feet, his tail sweeping across the floor in three-quarter time. You would have thought the dog had been born under our back porch. He was completely at home.

All I could do was shake my head. This was going to take all morning and I was sure Hayley was plenty busy at the shelter. Finally, I couldn't take it anymore. "Here, Todd, let me talk." I gently pulled the phone away and said, "This is George, Hayley. Let me help you."

"You already have, Mr. McCray—more than you know! Our adoption program is going very well this year and we repeatedly hear 'The McCrays sent us over.' Now Todd tells me that you are going to find homes for *all* the dogs in the shelter for the holiday. We're so pleased. That's wonderful!"

"Hayley, we'll help, but I doubt we can find homes for all of them. There must be dozens left."

"With your family's help, we're down to twenty-eight, not counting quarantine."

"Go over what you have and we'll see what we can do, but we can't promise the shelter will be emptied out by Christmas."

Hayley went over the inventory of remaining adoptable dogs as I made out the list. After we hung up, I turned to Todd. "You think about where we might be able to place some dogs and I have some work to do."

After replacing a frayed electrical line to the heater on the stock tank, I came back inside for breakfast and to check on Todd's progress. He had several pieces of paper and was trying to match up the dogs with prospective placements. He was up to line 14. His writing was deteriorating, but still legible. "Collee mix, geel, 7 . . . Merk and Cary."

As I headed in to wash up for breakfast, I considered putting a stop to this matchmaking. Perhaps this was getting out of hand. Having been placed in an uncomfortable position with this dog myself, why was I doing the same thing to my family and friends? I was also concerned that I was putting pressure on Todd. I looked in the mirror as I washed my hands and wondered what was the right thing to do. The man I saw didn't know either, but could smell sausage and biscuits cooking and coffee brewing. The sound of silverware and dishes being hurriedly placed on the table told me that breakfast was about ready.

After all these years of marriage, I still marveled at the way Mary Ann made breakfast come off the stove at the exact moment I turned the spigot off in that old sink.

We sat down to eat, but Todd ignored his food. He was back on the phone with Hayley, getting more details together on the dogs. It appeared that they were becoming friends.

"Yes, I named him Christmas. He's right here beneath my feet. We're going to find a home for each one."

"Todd!" I couldn't help interjecting. "Quit telling her that! We can't make that promise."

"I gotta go. My dad and I have lots of work to do." Todd hung up the receiver and smiled. I had never seen him happier. He wasn't feeling pressured—he was feeling the pure joy of doing the right thing. While I hadn't planned on spending my day finding temporary homes for dogs, my misgivings melted away as I, like Todd, caught the spirit of Christmas. I jumped right in.

"Hand me that list, Todd, and let's start matching some dogs up. Mary Ann, you just call these people and tell them about their dog, and ask when they can pick it up. Don't give them an opportunity to object or even think about it."

I noticed signs of protest on her face and headed her off. "This is a family project. Mary Ann, we need your help. Todd, what do you think about Hank? I'm sure he hasn't picked out a dog yet. Let's make it easy for him. You know a dairy farmer doesn't need a dog that barks a lot. Something older and steady would suit Hank best."

Todd looked up and down the list until he saw the perfect match for Hank. He scribbled Hank's name beside an entry for Sally. "Good choice?" he asked, flashing the list in front of my face.

"I remember that lazy old coonhound. She wouldn't even get up and walk over to see us. That's a perfect choice for old Hank. None better. What we need now is a closer. Somebody who can make the deal happen, someone with unparalleled powers of persuasion, like a debate coach. Do you know anyone who will not accept *no* for an answer?"

"You mean Mom?"

"Perfect. She's the one!" I turned abruptly to my wife and said, "Mary Ann, call Hank's wife and tell her it's a black and tan coonhound, female, twelve years old, likes all cows, but prefers Holsteins."

Mary Ann, it seemed, was also getting into the spirit. She moved toward the phone and resolutely began to dial the Fishers' number.

"Jean, this is Mary Ann. How are you this morning? Beautiful day, isn't it? Is Hank done with his milking? Sure glad you came by yesterday. Say, Jean, George and Todd were just talking to the shelter and I guess they have a coon dog over there named Sally that still needs a home." She paused and then went for the sale. "Are you and Hank still interested?"

There was a long pause and Todd and I began to wonder.

"Well, Jean, I'm sure George and Todd could pick her up for you and probably take her back too."

There was another pause and I moved closer to Mary Ann so I could hear the other end of the conversation. I could barely make out Jean's voice. It was backpedaling at its worst: "We don't have any dog food and we're going to be gone an awful lot of Christmas Day and Hank is worried about a strange dog bothering his cows."

I whispered to Mary Ann, "We'll buy the dog food."

She pushed me away and turned her back to me. For some reason, like all wives, Mary Ann did not like me talking to her while she was on the phone.

"Well, Jean, I do understand, you and Hank being at that point in your life. If you talk to Hank and he changes his mind, just give us a call. Merry Christmas."

Todd looked up at me, stupefied. "Dad, I don't understand. Hank changed his mind. Why wouldn't Hank want a dog for a few days?"

There may not have been an answer that Todd would accept. It wouldn't dawn on him that most of us tire of giving. "I don't know, son. Maybe he has too many cows." I knew that response was a fill-in-the-blank for most of us. If it wasn't too many cows, it was too many kids, too much work, or too many problems.

Although it was a hard lesson to learn, Todd was seeing for himself that there is seldom room at our own inn for others.

There were two more calls that did not go well, either. I was beginning to wonder if this family project was going to work. Something inside me told me to leave it alone for now, but Todd would have none of that.

"Jonathan will take the dogs. You call him. I know he will."

I called the number and spoke with my daughter-in-law.

"Karen, this is George. We sure enjoyed seeing you and the boys last night. I hope you had a good time."

"Oh, George, we had a great time. The kids are still buzzing around here talking about the Christmas dog."

"Really?" I said, hoping she would volunteer more information without me having to ask.

"Yes. In fact, the boys and Jonathan are on their way to the shelter as we speak."

"Say, Karen, would you mind repeating that to Todd? He's right here and I think he would like to hear it too."

"Sure," she said and I passed the receiver.

The two of them spoke for a few moments and Todd was clearly pleased by his big brother's commitment.

Another call revealed that my daughter, Hannah, had apparently spent the morning sneaking a rather skittish German short-haired pointer named Baron from his cage and up into her apartment, where pets were not allowed. She was certain, however, that this rule did not apply to temporary houseguests. Being a well-educated accountant, she knows all about rules and contracts. Todd and I were sure she was right.

By December 22 our family members had taken twelve dogs. Our neighbors and friends had taken several more, but there were still seventeen dogs left in the shelter and we were out of prospects.

Todd didn't seem worried. He grabbed the phone book and said he had a call or two to make. I left him alone as he headed to the barn. He returned an hour later with a big smile on his face and, though uncertain, I suspected that he convinced either the governor or the state legislature to adopt the remaining inhabitants of the Cherokee County Animal Shelter. The next vehicle that turned into our drive that day solved the mystery.

Around two-thirty that afternoon, a television van found its way, with Todd's help, to our rural home. I had seen it at the courthouse before with a big "5" on the side and the satellite antenna on top. At first, I thought it was lost or there had been an accident on the highway not far from our house, but then a woman I recognized as an anchor from channel 5 came to the front door.

Todd yelled out, "Someone must be selling something!"

"No, it's a television truck."

"Oh, that's for me," Todd said calmly.

It was then that I realized what Todd had been doing on the phone. We all went to the front door and welcomed our local celebrity with anxious glances. She introduced herself as Brenda Lewis and asked for Todd, who immediately stepped up and held out his hand.

She smiled at him. "It's nice to meet you in person, Todd. The station manager and I enjoyed talking with you this morning and we decided to follow your suggestion and do a story on the Adopt a Dog for Christmas program. Can we come in and talk with you about it?"

"Yes, come in, please."

We sat on the sofa, by the fire. Brenda Lewis talked to Todd and shook Christmas's paw and then asked me if I could turn up the volume on the Nat King Cole Christmas music Mary Ann had been listening to. Motioning to the cameraman, she began to tell her audience all about Adopt a Dog for Christmas. The camera panned to our family and Christmas on the sofa as she described Todd's efforts. She told her viewers that the shelter was staying open late that night and would be open tomorrow morning until noon. As she walked to the end of the living room, the cameraman followed her and pointed the camera at all of the decorations in our house. She finished by saying in her best anchor voice, "Let's all do what we can so Todd's dream can come true. Please adopt a dog for Christmas!"

The television crew shook our hands, told us the story would air at six o'clock and ten o'clock, and left. Naturally, we called everyone we knew to tell them that Todd would be on the news. Todd called Hayley at the shelter; she couldn't believe her ears. The day seemed to drag on slowly as we carefully checked our watches to make sure we did not miss Todd's marketing efforts. Finally, at six PM, Todd, Christmas, Mary Ann, and I all piled on the sofa and watched Brenda Lewis on the evening news. From that day forward, Todd became a great fan of channel 5.

Around seven o'clock, after dinner, Jonathan and his kids arrived to show us their dogs. My grandsons were as excited as I had ever seen them. Everyone had watched the news and was kidding Todd about being a television celebrity. He seemed quiet and I thought something was bothering him. It's not often that a young man like Todd can make a big difference in even one little corner of the world. The ten o'clock segment was the same as the six o'clock. Mary Ann and I went to bed excited and proud that our son and his adopted dog were now both famous.

Christmas Eve arrived and chores still needed to be done. I came in through the back door. Todd was sprawled out on the kitchen floor, with Christmas snuggled up beside him. His headphones were on and his eyes were closed. I waited a few minutes, took off my hat and gloves, sat down at the kitchen table, and said loud enough for him to hear,

"Good morning, Todd. Missed you for chores today. What are you doing?"

He took his headphones off, stood up, and sat down with me at the table without saying a word. He folded his hands in his lap.

"What's wrong, Todd? Do you feel all right?"

"Yeah, I was just wondering if all the other dogs were adopted."

"Me too. Let's call Hayley and find out."

I waited for several rings but there was no answer. Had they decided to close early? I was about to hang up when Hayley, out of breath, answered the phone.

"Cherokee County Animal Shelter, Hayley speaking."

"Hayley, this is George and Todd."

"George, we placed *all* the remaining dogs this morning! It's been chaos. Our phones have been ringing off the hook. This friend of yours, the dairy farmer . . ."

"You mean Hank?" I interrupted. Todd had heard Hayley's news and was beaming.

"That's him. He was the first one in line this morning when we opened the doors. He took two!"

Todd pumped the air with his fist and yelled out to his mother, "Hank took two dogs! We did it! Every dog in the shelter is gone!" Christmas began to bark excitedly as Mary Ann came rushing in. She, Todd, and Christmas did a little victory dance.

"Thanks for everything, George. You and Todd did a good deed for our dogs."

Feeling a little embarrassed, I wanted Hayley to know that I had nothing to do with it. I called out to Todd in a voice Hayley could hear, "You did a good job, Todd."

I was going to wish Hayley a merry Christmas when she spoke again, but with a slightly disappointed tone. "Well, George, I said we found a place for all the dogs we had, but that's not quite right. We still have one in quarantine. A female. You don't have to tell Todd. I can come back tomorrow and feed her. It's okay. I don't want him to think he let us down. I know he tried so hard to find a home for all of the dogs."

"Can you stay open for another hour?" I asked.

"There is something you should know before you head down here, George."

"What?"

"She is about to have puppies."

CHAPTER 8

We could see deer in the meadow beyond the house and hear a hoot owl's cry from the barnyard. But what I remember most about that afternoon was the exciting chill that lingered in the air beneath a cloudless sky. Something special was happening in our corner of the universe. Mary Ann, Todd, Christmas, and I were all crammed into the cab of my truck. We were headed to the shelter to get the last unadopted dog in Cherokee County, Kansas. I called Jonathan and he agreed to come out with his boys and help fix up a place in the barn for our newest guest. They had been planning to come for dinner and to open presents, but now they showed up early and got to work. As we left, they were dragging heat lamps out of the garage and rummaging through the house for old blankets and bowls.

"Maybe we should just get into the shelter business," I

joked as we pulled out of our driveway. Todd seemed a little too pleased with that idea, so I had to add, "I'm kidding. Shelters don't get paid for keeping dogs. They are not a money-making business."

He looked confused, so I tried to explain. "They are like a charity. There is no one to pay for keeping the dogs. The dogs don't have owners to make payments."

He still looked puzzled. Before I realized it, I'd gone too far. "The dogs don't have homes. That's why they are at the shelter. Do you understand?"

Todd was quiet. I thought Hayley had explained this to him before, but the only thing that sunk in was that the shelter kept lots of dogs. Until now, he had not quite figured out how or why the dogs got there. Finally, as he sorted it out in his mind, he asked, "Why don't the dogs have owners?"

Trying again to help him understand, I said, "It's hard to say. Some people buy a dog and it just doesn't work out. Some people have to spend lots of time taking care of themselves and don't have anything left to share with an animal. You're not like that, though, are you?"

"No," he said slowly.

"I admire that about you, Todd." It was then that I knew what made someone an animal lover.

"Dad, what will happen to Christmas when we take him back?"

"He'll stay at the shelter until a very special person is willing to make Christmas a permanent part of his life."

"How long do you think that it will take?"

"The good ones go quickly, Todd. Maybe you could help Hayley find a home for him or, if you miss him, you can always go into town and visit."

Todd didn't say a word and I had no way of knowing if what I had said to him made any sense, or if it had been wise to suggest he visit Christmas after we returned him.

When we arrived, Hayley was pleased to see us, but surprised by the size of our entourage. She led us quickly into the shelter and down an empty corridor of cages. There was an eerie ghost-town feeling in the air. At the far end of the rows, we found the most recent addition and last remaining guest of the county animal shelter, a female dachshund the shelter employees named Ruthie.

Mary Ann opened the cage door. Her maternal instincts were ramped up to full power. She scooped up Ruthie before Todd and I could make an introduction. Ruthie eagerly greeted Mary Ann's face with her cold nose and it was clear that these two were going to be pals. We filled out the obligatory paperwork, bid Hayley a merry Christmas, and were quickly back on the road.

Todd and Christmas were the first victims of Mary Ann's newly found friendship with Ruthie. They were displaced to the back of the truck, where they huddled beneath a blanket to protect them from the chilly air as we headed home. Ruthie sat on Mary Ann's lap with a minimal amount of fidgeting.

Mary Ann and I hummed along with the Christmas

tunes that played on the radio and we both felt truly happy. Mary Ann's hand reached over to touch my cheek and then rested gently on Ruthie. This was a Christmas Eve to remember.

As I turned the truck into our driveway, we could see activity in the barn and knew that Jonathan and the kids were preparing for our newest Christmas guest. Driving past the house, I went through an open gate and directly into the barnyard. Mary Ann cradled Ruthie protectively as we got out of the truck and walked to the barn.

"Hello!" Jonathan called out as we opened the barn door. "Come see what we've done."

One of the large box stalls that had housed Dick and Doc, the draft horses that pulled the maintainer years ago, was now our makeshift maternity ward. Within it, they had made a box with two-by-twelve boards and lined it with straw. A heat lamp hung from the rafters and some old towels were in the corner. Jonathan brought out a lawn chair from the garage, where he remained perched while his boys hammered in a few more nails. Mary Ann stepped over the sides of the box and gently set Ruthie on the bed of towels.

We had hosted many animal births on this farm and had learned to respect nature as a good midwife. We provided our moms privacy and they did the rest. Christmas jumped over the boards, sniffed Ruthie, and then curled down beside her, gently nudging her face and ears with his nose. She would have none of it. She growled and Christmas wisely backed off. However comfortable with humans

Ruthie may have been, she wanted no part of an unknown male dog, at least at this point.

Mary Ann scolded the poor dog. "You men just don't know when to keep your distance, do you?"

Once our guest was settled to Todd's and Mary Ann's satisfaction, we headed back to the house for a family dinner. We ate quickly, as all of us were more concerned with Ruthie than with having another helping of mashed potatoes. After dinner, Nurse Mary Ann led the procession back down to the nursery for another inspection. She made the men stand in the cold night air while she went in with Jonathan's wife, Karen. When they came out of the barn, Jonathan's youngest son, Jeremy, looked up behind eager eyes. "Grandma, can we open presents now?"

Mary Ann lifted Jeremy up and held him close. "It's time," she announced, glancing back at the barn door. "Shut the door," she called out as she carried Jeremy back to the house.

I don't remember any of the presents that I gave or received that year. Truth was I seldom gave or received anything that was truly needed. It was after eight PM by the time all the presents were opened and the children were loaded back into the car.

After Jonathan and his family left, I snapped the red lead onto Christmas's green collar and took him outside and waited patiently for him to do his business. We watched as Todd and Mary Ann went down to the barn to check once again on Ruthie. Christmas seemed strangely agitated, restless. He pulled on his leash and whined, and barked once or twice in the direction of the woods that flanked Kill Creek. I suspected that there were deer in the nearby meadow.

Todd and Mary Ann joined me and reported that Ruthie was resting comfortably. Walking to the house, Christmas pulled, and though he came along, he stopped in the doorway, turned toward the barn, and barked again, not happy about what was left behind.

"What's wrong, Christmas?" I asked. "Isn't the Hilton good enough for you anymore?" We were apparently too exhausted to notice the open barn door.

CHAPTER 9

I was in the deepest of sleep when a different kind of Christmas clatter woke me late in the night. It was not Santa on the roof. It was a Christmas dog barking and throwing himself at the back door with the full force of his body. Todd was screaming, "Dad, Dad, something is wrong with Christmas!" Dogs have a wide variety of barks. Some barks are meant to warn, others to intimidate, but not this bark. It was a higher-pitched bark that seemed to be highly agitated and concerned. Trying to focus, I listened more closely and could make out Ruthie's high-pitched bark. Something or someone was in the barn and that couldn't be good.

Mary Ann and I both pulled on our robes and I decided to take no chances. My grandfather was right. It was good to have a gun in the house. I rummaged through the bottom of the closet and found the ancient rifle I had hoped I would never need. I chambered a round, grabbed an extra bullet, and headed down the stairs as fast as I could on a leg that was still cold and stiff.

By the time I got to the door, Todd had opened it and Christmas streaked out with more speed than I could have imagined. He stretched into full flight. It seemed as if his feet did not bother touching the ground. I followed behind, moving as fast as I could, but unable to match the dog's quick exit. Mary Ann was yelling behind us all, "Be careful!"

Ruthie was barking more urgently from the barn. Then there was snarling, hissing, and an awful racket of unfamiliar sounds. "Todd!" I hollered. "Don't you dare go into that barn!"

Christmas did not hesitate. As he shot into the barn, his barks became even more intense before turning into snarls. Within seconds, there was a sound I had heard only a few times in my life. It was the unmistakable din of animal warriors locked in a life-or-death battle. The noise was horrific and unyielding. The sounds suggested that nothing could possibly be living in that barn within a very few short moments. Would Todd know to stay out of a fight like this? He still had not reached the barn. I had to do something quickly.

I raised my rifle and fired into the air, hoping to frighten away this intruder or maybe scare Todd enough to slow him down. The old rifle has quite a kick to it and the shot caused an immediate ringing in my ear. I ejected the spent cartridge and chambered the one remaining round. Though I had not fired a gun since 1969, the motions came easily to me, without thinking.

Just as Todd came to the barn door, swinging open in the wind, a flash of brown exploded from the door and nearly knocked him over. I could not believe my eyes. It was a full-grown cougar making a run for it. Todd was right. It was a darn big cat and it moved with a grace and power that I had never witnessed in man or animal.

Christmas was after him with the zeal born of centuries of breeding. He barked and Todd screamed and all three of them were headed across the barnyard. The big cat came to the fence and, instead of leaping over, spun around and faced Christmas as he closed in.

A motion detector caused the barn's floodlights to turn on and I could see the cat hissing and pawing at the air as Christmas danced from side to side, forward and backward, with a menacing growl. The cat would approach and Christmas would back off. When the cat retreated slightly, Christmas would again lunge forward, only to be rebuffed again. The cat was growing more aggressive and suddenly it crouched and leaped forward to close the gap. With one giant swipe, he smacked Christmas across the chest with his right paw. Christmas was flicked like a fly from a tabletop and tossed five feet through the air. He rolled back onto his feet and angrily attacked again, oblivious to the size and skill of his foe.

While I hoped that Todd would know better than to get

in the middle of a fight like this, amid the excitement, I was not sure. It was with him, therefore, that my worry remained. Leaning against the barn for support, I trained the gun sight on the big cat. He was fifty yards out and it would be a difficult shot, particularly with Todd and Christmas moving in and out of my line of fire.

"Todd," I yelled. "Get to the ground so I can shoot the rifle." He must have been too excited, for he kept going. Disaster was only moments away and I had to take a chance on one shot. My mind sifted through the options quickly. It came across my mind that the easiest shot would be to Todd's leg. It just might save his life. I also thought about the dog. I was sure that the cat would leave on his own but for the attacking dog. The cat was the hardest shot of the three, but I knew it was the only one I could live with myself for taking. I again tried to put the cat in the sight, but he was still moving too quickly. I had no confidence in my ability to make that shot, particularly with such an old rifle. Wounding the animal could make things worse. By eliminating his ability to run away, he would be forced to stand and fight.

The shot needed to be a clean kill. I needed another option and came up with it. I did not like it, but I could not think of anything else to do.

Aiming, I slowly squeezed the trigger. The old .30-06 jumped in my arms and the recoil threw me back. The crack rang out over Cherokee County like an explosion. Todd froze, pulled back into reality. The bullet struck the gravel in the few feet between the cougar and the dog. Rocks and stones spewed up into the faces of both beasts. I lowered the rifle.

I knew I had only an instant while the dog's concentration was broken and I yelled at the top of my lungs, "Christmas."

When he turned in my direction, I then screamed the one order we had practiced the last several days. "Sit!" I pushed the air down with the palm of my hand.

Christmas looked at me, and while he did not obey the command, he was distracted. The big cat took advantage of the lull, turned, gathered his strength, and leaped over the fence.

Christmas, seeing the escape, ran along the fence line, searching for an opening. Todd and I yelled at him, but it was no use. He squeezed through and, with the yelps of a hound, set out in the darkness after the cat.

Quickly both animals passed through the meadow, out of the range of our lights, and into the surrounding forest. I figured the cat would leave Christmas far behind in no time.

"Todd, are you okay? Let's check the barn." He hesitated, staring at the fence where Christmas had disappeared, but turned and came back toward me. I was panting and out of breath before I got to the barn door. Mary Ann was at my elbow as I turned on the inside light. We were scared to death for Ruthie. She was huddled in the corner. Mary Ann cautiously approached her motionless body. Not having the nerve to look, I stayed back.

Mary Ann let out an excited scream. "Three of them!"

Ruthie had managed to give birth to three puppies that were suckling beside her.

"Three puppies," I repeated.

Before we could head back to bed, Christmas ambled back to the barn, where we had remained with Ruthie, as if he had been on a casual midnight stroll. Despite the swat he'd taken from the cougar, remarkably, he was unharmed except for a few scratches.

Todd put his arms around the dog's neck. "That was a big cat, Dad! Not too big for Christmas, though, was it?"

"Nope. I guess you were right, Todd. No cat is too big for Christmas."

Mary Ann turned to me. "I've had enough excitement for one night. Let's leave Ruthie to be with her puppies. Morning will be here soon enough."

Before walking back to the house, we checked and rechecked to make sure the barn door was closed.

Todd headed immediately to bed. Mary Ann and I fell into the two big stuffed chairs that flank the fireplace, our hearts still beating from the excitement. Christmas also seemed unsettled. He sat between us and pawed at my knee. "So, you want to be petted?" I asked. "I guess you deserve it. You are one amazing dog." He let out a little whimper and then settled down to sleep.

CHAPTER 10

The next day brought us a holiday to remember. I was a little late with the chores, but Todd, Mary Ann, and I made hourly visits to the barn to check on Ruthie and the puppies. None of the scratches the big cat inflicted on Christmas was serious, but still Todd dabbed the cuts with iodine. Hayley called from her house and insisted on driving out to the farm to see the litter. Upon her arrival, Todd showed her each puppy and recounted last night's heroics. I was not sure whether she was more impressed with Todd's ability to handle animals or Christmas's ability to handle cougars.

She waited for the right moment and then pulled me aside and whispered, "George, after Christmas, would you please call me? I'd like to discuss Todd with you. We might have a job for him at the shelter. We have an opening, but

I've been slow to fill it. I've been waiting for the right person to apply. I think I may have found him."

"I can't think of a nicer Christmas present for Todd," I said. While nodding in agreement, I decided to not say anything to Todd or his mother until after the twenty-sixth. I wanted to deal with the issue of returning Christmas first.

Later that morning, the channel 5 news truck pulled up to do a follow-up story on the puppies and the Adopt a Dog for Christmas program. Brenda Lewis took a picture of Todd, Mary Ann, and me, each of us holding a puppy, with Christmas and Ruthie looking on like proud parents. It now sits in a frame on our mantel.

When the news crew was finished with us, they turned down the road to do a segment on Hank. It seemed that he was doing just fine with his two dogs.

Christmas Day was thankfully calm. Two of my grandchildren phoned Todd several times to pass on the anecdotal happenings of their adopted Christmas dogs. Todd, in turn, updated them on our excitement. It seemed that notwithstanding my efforts, we had been added to the list of local crackpots claiming to have seen a cougar but having absolutely no proof except for the temporary iodine stains on Christmas's fur.

For lunch, Mary Ann warmed up leftovers and then we relaxed for the rest of the day, doing little more than feeling the winter sun as it poured through the window, putting logs on the fire, and enjoying our four-legged guests. We were all tired from the previous day's excitement and allowed ourselves to nap, with our dog curled up beside us.

That night we rested our heads on pillows and let the bed take over the job of supporting our tired bodies. Mary Ann leaned over, kissed me softly on the cheek, and said, "Merry Christmas, George."

I held her tightly, not only because I loved her dearly but also because I wanted to hold the moment—my most memorable Christmas. "Merry Christmas, Mary Ann."

"George?" she asked softly. "What are you going to do with Christmas tomorrow?"

I took her hand, massaging her fingers gently, and told her truthfully, "I don't know." There was nothing I wanted more than to just tell Todd that Christmas was staying, but that still did not sit right with me. At that particular moment, I couldn't explain that what I wanted to give Todd was a gift more important than a dog. I didn't know how to explain that the gift with the most love cannot always be wrapped or delivered. I didn't know if Mary Ann could accept that some of the best gifts for Todd would not be given but withheld. I knew exactly what I should do; I just didn't know how to do it. Nor did I particularly want to do it. There was no doubt in my mind that letting him keep the dog would be the easiest thing to do.

It was one of those confounding times when I did not know whether the bigger man held his ground or just let go and admitted he was wrong.

On December 26 I awoke to a bright, clear day with frost on the ground. Todd was already in the barn when I went out to do the chores. Christmas was with him. Sitting in the lawn chair, Todd held a tiny puppy in his hands. He,

Christmas, Ruthie, and the puppies had all come together on our small farm. For a moment they were family. I didn't have the strength to tell them that it couldn't last. I turned around and went back to the house before any of them noticed me watching from the door.

After breakfast, Todd came to me. "I called Hayley. She is going to come out and help us with the puppies and Ruthie."

I looked over the top of my newspaper. "That's good, Todd."

"Dad?"

"Yes, Todd." I was bracing for what was coming next.

"About Christmas . . ." he started.

"Yes?"

To my surprise, and in a matter-of-fact way, he plunged ahead. "It's the twenty-sixth and we have to take him back. That's the way the program works. You take the dogs back on the twenty-sixth."

I looked to Mary Ann, suspecting she was losing the fight against her tears. A few small ones rolled down her cheeks. I thought it would be Todd crying.

Things like this never happen in any one instant, but right there, I knew that Todd had taken a giant leap toward becoming a man. He had learned something so important: He kept his word, even when he could make no sense out of the commitment. Putting my arms around Todd, I said, "That's right, son. That's how the program works. It's a good program too. Isn't it?"

Later that morning, Hayley arrived to pick up Ruthie and the puppies and Todd left me to help her. She didn't say anything about taking Christmas and we didn't mention it either. I stayed away, still cursing myself, uncertain of my decision and feeling a little bit sorry for myself. It happened again. I was attached to this dog and now I was going to lose him, just like Tucker and Charlie. Alone in the barn, I sat on the milking stool and stewed. There was still no good answer.

When I got back to the house, Todd was waiting for me. He was sitting on the porch in his tattered blue jeans and red tennis shoes, listening to his radio. He was humming softly to Christmas tunes. When I walked up to him, he just smiled, patted Christmas on the head, snapped the green leash onto his red collar, and headed out to the truck. Christmas did not complain or resist. He jumped into the cab and the two of them waited patiently while I fumbled for my keys, trying to come up with some rational way to avoid this heartbreak.

It was a very long ride into town that morning. Todd did not once ask me to reconsider our agreement to return Christmas. He just sat patiently, with his headphones on, one arm wrapped protectively around Christmas.

Today was December 26 and, as promised, Christmas was going back to the shelter. I was never more proud of Todd, nor more irritated with myself. Todd was on the road to becoming an adult. I wasn't so sure what road I was on. When we arrived at the shelter, Todd jumped out of the truck and Christmas followed, but when I hesitated, Todd peered into the truck. "Don't worry, I'll take Christmas inside for you."

Todd slammed the truck door shut and headed toward the entrance. When Todd opened the front door of the shelter, Christmas stopped, turned, and looked back at me. I leaned across the seat and reached for the passenger door. I wanted to open it, to call them back, to put an end to this. Again, I tried to toughen up. I had asked Todd to be a man and I would not take this accomplishment away from him, no matter how hard it was on me. So, I just sat, waited, and felt miserable. After a few minutes, Hayley and Todd came out together. Hayley came around to the driver's side, and I rolled the window down.

She patted my arm and said, "Don't worry, Mr. McCray, we'll take good care of him."

"Thanks," was all I could say. I looked over at Todd. He already had his headphones on, retreating into his own world. Forcing myself, I put the truck in reverse and headed home.

There must have been ten times when I started to think about places to turn around and go back and get that dog, but I kept the truck heading west until I saw our farm on the horizon. In a few days we would all feel better.

CHAPTER 11

Mary Ann tried to be patient with me. She knew I was trying my hardest to do what was best for Todd and not just what was easy, but for the next few days, it might have been warmer outside than standing beside the arctic blast formerly known as my wife. Todd called Hayley and checked on Christmas and Ruthie several times a day and learned that they were fine.

On December 29, Hayley called and asked for me. I assumed she was calling about the job she had mentioned, but I didn't want to get my hopes up for Todd.

"So," I said, "I hear that Christmas is doing well."

"He is indeed. I just wanted to thank you and your family for all you did. The program was a huge success this year. I think all of the families had such a good time with their guests. Over half the families kept their dogs, which means we aren't so cramped."

"Over half kept their dogs?" I repeated, stunned. "Really? But I thought most everyone brought their dogs back. I thought that was how the program worked."

"Of course, we don't want anyone to keep a dog they don't want, but if a family likes the dog and meets our requirements for pet ownership, then we are pleased to place it."

I was silent as her words sunk in. In my determination to teach Todd a lesson, it hadn't occurred to me that most people would keep their dogs. This seemed to make returning Christmas to the shelter even worse. Finally, I just said, "I guess I had it all wrong."

"No, there is no right or wrong, George. Just what works for your family. By the way, we are thinking about adding cats to the program next year!"

"Humm," I muttered.

"Say, George, I wanted to talk to you about the job at the shelter. We would like to offer Todd the position. It doesn't pay much, but I bet he would really like it. He's so good with animals. They trust him. What do you think?"

What I thought was, *I must be dreaming.* I was so happy for Todd and pleased that someone besides his mother and me could recognize just how much he had to offer. I had always hoped that Todd would someday have a real job and some normalcy in his life. I wanted to scream for joy, but I just collected myself and smiled at Mary Ann, who had initially answered the phone and stayed in the kitchen. She looked at me, puzzled, and could sense my excitement. I

whispered to her, "The shelter is offering Todd a job."
Again, poor Mary Ann was crying.

"When can he start?" I asked Hayley.

"Is Monday morning too soon?"

"What time?"

"Seven forty-five should work. The shelter opens at eight o'clock."

"We'll be there, Hayley! And thanks so much."

"George, just one more thing . . ."

"Yes, Hayley?"

"There have been two families wanting to adopt Christmas. One claims that he's their dog who had apparently wandered off months ago. They said that they recognized him from the news story that was picked up in other parts of the state. I told them that Christmas was on hold for a few days because the adoptive families always get first dibs. Should I let him go?"

"Hayley, let me think on it," I said, my elation for Todd turning to something else. I still did not know what to do.

"I'll wait until closing time today, five PM, but no longer."

"Thanks for everything. Mary Ann and I are so pleased and we think that there isn't a soul in the universe that could do a better job with the shelter's dogs than Todd. You can count on it. You will not be disappointed."

"I'm sure you are right, George."

"Hayley, I'll get back to you on the dog."

"No problem."

When I hung up the receiver I was so excited I hardly knew what to do. Mary Ann and I danced around the room until I felt the need to say, "I told you so."

She dropped her embrace. "What do you mean by that?"

"Trying to teach Todd to be like an adult has paid off. Bringing the dog back. That's what I mean. It all turned out right."

"George McCray, don't you dare try to take one bit of credit for this. This is all Todd's doing. You're still an old fool for not keeping that dog."

I suspected she was right, but of course there is nothing more infuriating than being married to someone who is right, which caused me to lash out. "Well, I sure hope the shelter doesn't need someone to climb more than two rungs high on a ladder or to drive a truck out of first gear."

As soon as the words were out of my mouth, I knew the comment was unfair. Rightly so, Mary Ann stormed out of the kitchen.

Not to be overshadowed by her indignation, I slammed the back door and looked around the barnyard for Todd. He was probably out exploring, for he was nowhere to be found. I decided to get in the truck and visit Hank. He would be so excited for Todd. Besides, Hank often had a way of making sense out of things that were too troubling for the milk stool.

Hank was down at his barn doing what farmers spend most of their time doing: fixing the machinery that is supposed to make their lives easier. A lot of wisdom can pass while holding a wrench for Hank. He was replacing some worn sprockets on a hay elevator and chomping on the un-lit stub of a cigar when I found him. He spat occasionally and laughed as I recounted the adventure of the cougar.

"Cougar?" he asked suspiciously.

It seemed that his coonhound had worked out just fine. He did return the other dog, concluding that one was enough. He told me that Sally was the best equipment purchase he had made in years. Free. I then turned to the subject of Todd.

"It's like this, Hank. I want Todd to be responsible more than I want him to have a dog. With this job at the shelter, he'll be around dogs all day."

"Makes sense, George. Would you hand me that can of WD-40?"

I passed him the can and he sprayed the solvent on a frozen three-quarter-inch nut that would not budge. I continued. "Todd getting this job is a big step in the right direction. Me caving in seems like the wrong way to go."

Hank grunted and the nut came loose from the bolt. "Sounds like you're trying to convince yourself of something. What are you so worried about?"

I looked at him with surprise and he knew he was going to have to say more to make his point. I pressed him. "What do you mean?"

"Are you sure this is not more about you and less about Todd than you think?"

"What?" I asked again, still confused.

"Maybe I'm wrong, George, but Todd having this dog or

not having this dog isn't going to make an iota of difference in the long run. At least not to Todd." He looked me straight in the eye. "Getting the dog would be good for you, George."

"How's that?"

"George, you spend your life taking care of things. That's a farmer's life. You take care of fences, animals, equipment, and plants. You nurture and bring things to life. Like your dad and your grandfather before you, you're a good farmer, a good father, and a good husband." He chuckled and then added, "And a darn good neighbor. The problem is, George, that you've become so comfortable giving to others that you forgot how to let something or someone give back to you. For some reason it makes you uncomfortable. Ever since you've come back from that war, George, you don't want anyone doing anything for you. Why is that?"

Hank might as well have struck me on the side of my head with that wrench he was holding. "Honestly, Hank, I never thought this had a thing to do with me."

Hank grunted and spat a little more cigar out onto the barn floor. "Would you hand me that wire brush over there?" He handed me the wrench and took the brush. "George, this has everything to do with you and absolutely nothing to do with Todd. Get that through your head." He spat out one more bit of tobacco. "But, I suppose I could be wrong."

We both knew he was right. I stayed a little longer handing Hank tools and watching his breath condense in the cool winter air. I handed him another brush, a mallet, and a screwdriver. Finally, I knew that I needed to go home.

"Sure you don't want to stay for a cup of coffee?" he asked.

"No. Thanks. I have some dog business to attend to."

He clasped my arm. "Good for you, George."

As I drove back to the house, I made up my mind. I needed a way to fix everything without compromising and without teaching Todd a lesson I did not want him to learn. Hank's words gave me the inspiration I needed.

When I got back to the house, Todd was sitting on the back porch. His radio was playing and his hands were pushed deep into his coat pockets. My legs ached as I got out of the truck and slowly made my way over to him.

I sat down beside him. "Son, would you take off your earphones for a minute?"

"Sure, Dad."

"Hayley called."

"I know I have a job. Start Monday."

He smiled at me and started to put his headphones back on.

"Todd, would you please keep your headphones off? I was thinking, with you having a job of your own now, things might get a little lonely around here for me."

"Yeah, you're losing your helper, aren't you?"

"Are you okay with that?"

"Sure," he said. "The shelter pays better than you." He then started to put his headphones back on again.

I reached out and grabbed his wrist. "Todd, you know how I have always thought dogs don't work out well for me?"

"Yeah," he said.

"After Christmas, I don't think that anymore."

Todd smiled. "I am a good dog picker, aren't I?"

"I was thinking maybe I need a dog too. A new helper. What do you think?"

"Sure," he said, "but only if you clean your room first." He chuckled and I playfully punched his arm.

"Todd, I was thinking maybe Christmas would be a good dog for me. What do you think?"

He looked at me with a very blank face. I think he was too frozen with excitement to show any expression. He jumped up. "I'll get the leash! You get the keys!"

"I'll get the collar too!" I pushed open the back door and looked for Mary Ann. She was brutalizing some poor, defenseless biscuit dough with a rolling pin. I had a feeling that those little protrusions in the mound of dough were substituting for my own facial features.

She turned to me and curtly asked, "What?"

Todd pushed in behind me and stuck his head in between my arms so I could hold him in a headlock. I gently spun him around so he could see his mother. "Tell your mom what we decided."

"Dad needs a dog, Mom, 'cause I got a job and can't help with the chores as much."

Mary Ann looked skeptically at us both and tried to figure out what we were up to. "Really?" she asked. "And when did that happen?"

"Just now," Todd said.

I tightened my grip slightly with my right hand and then rubbed a few of Todd's ribs and asked, "How good can you tell Mom what dog we're getting when I am tickling you like this?" I strummed his ribs like an old guitar.

Todd laughed and squirmed and said, "Dad wants Christmas, Mom. He is going to be Dad's dog now."

For the second time in a day, Mary Ann was crying, but this time she was in my arms and I could feel her sweet kisses. "Oh, George, you finally understand that it was you that needed the dog, don't you?"

"Yeah, it was me."

"Well, what are you doing just standing here? Get to town!"

I took a long drink of water from a tin cup that I kept by the sink, grinned at Mary Ann, and then pushed Todd out the door.

CHAPTER 12

Mr. Conner considered it unlikely that the dog on the television was Jake, but he would never forgive himself if he did not make the one-hour drive over to Cherokee County to find out. His children and grandchildren told him that they knew Jake when they saw Jake. Mr. Conner told the children that Cherokee County was more than sixty miles away and that dogs did not typically roam that far from home. Mr. Conner's children swore up and down that it had to be Jake. He was inclined to attribute the Jake sighting to wishful thinking. For, after all, he told them, there are more than a few big black dogs around. But to satisfy his own curiosity, he decided to check it out. Besides, he concluded, the worst-case scenario was a quiet drive in the country.

Conner smiled and thought about the old dog. It sounded like Jake's business was serious this time. He had managed to get himself on television as the champion of a noble cause. What other dog could do that? He wondered about Jake's new family and why they brought him back to the shelter. The shelter manager told him that the family that kept the dog over Christmas had a few things to work out before they made a final adoption decision. If they did not want Jake, then he could claim the dog after the shelter officially closed at five PM. Hayley said he could show up anytime after five but before five-thirty, while the staff was feeding the animals and preparing to close for the night.

According to Hayley, yet another family was interested in Jake too, but if the dog was Jake, as former owners they would have a higher priority. Mr. Conner checked his watch. He was early. He did not mind. This way, he would have a chance to see if it was Jake, and if it wasn't, he could turn around and be home before the traffic was bad.

Mr. Conner pulled up behind an old brown Ford pickup truck that was moving way too slowly, put on his blinker, and passed it. He marveled at the distances between homes and wondered how these rural inhabitants got by without a grocery store, video store, coffee shop, laundry, or deli within easy driving distance.

Around four-thirty, Conner pulled into the Cherokee County seat, a small town called Crossing Trails. He had to chuckle when he saw that the main street was actually called Main Street.

Conner fumbled for the directions and quickly determined that he needed to pass through the square and turn south on Prairie Center Road. When the light turned green, he pulled forward and tried to make out the worn street signs. When he found Prairie Center, he turned right, and within forty yards the pavement turned to gravel. He checked his watch again. It was 4:40. He followed the gravel road past a less-than-spectacular neighborhood until he finally came upon an old building that was clearly marked as the Cherokee County Animal Shelter.

It was time to find out about this dog. Conner collected his wallet and car keys, walked to the front door, opened it, and then looked around for assistance in a reception area that had been taken over by outdated office furniture. Seeing no one around, he pushed past a swinging door and into the animal holding area. Two shelter employees seemed to be in a heated discussion. Conner approached them and waited for a pause to interrupt.

CHAPTER 13

"Todd, you drive to town this time," I said as I handed Todd the keys to the truck. "Now that you have a job, you need to get more driving practice in, so you can take yourself to work. I can't be running you in every day."

"Are you sure?" he asked.

"Why not? Now that you are a high-salaried government employee, maybe you'll make enough money to have a car of your own."

"Do we have to stay in first gear the whole way?"

"Nah, as soon as we get over the hill where your mom can't see, shift into second."

I probably did not pick the best time for driving practice, but I was so ready for Todd to start growing up that I rushed things when I should have known better. Sure, I had let Todd drive on the highway a few times before. Over his mother's objections, he earned his learner's permit a few years ago, but had never received his unrestricted license. But concentrating on the dog business and concentrating on his driving business at the same time was presenting a few problems. More than once, I had to reach over and make sure he did not stray over into the other lane.

"Todd, I think we are going to have to do some practicing."

"You think so, Dad?" he asked.

"It's real important, Todd, that you stay right in your lane."

"Somebody is behind me, Dad." I turned around and looked. Sure enough, a red Ford decided to use the highway that day too. I waved him around us and he passed, disappearing ahead of us. He had out-of-county tags and probably wondered why in the world we were driving so slowly.

When we got to Crossing Trails, Todd did a real nice job at the stoplight and then turned down the road to the shelter.

"You're doing just fine, Todd. I think you are a good driver. Very safe. Your mom would be very proud of you and so am I."

"Never had an accident," he proudly noted.

Stifling my laughter, I said, "Yep, you're pitching a perfect game so far. Let's keep it up, okay?"

There were only a few cars in the lot, but two things seemed out of place. The red Ford that passed us on the highway was now sitting in the lot, and someone had placed one of those large construction trailers on the edge of the property.

Todd had no problem parking my truck. It was 4:45, so we made it in plenty of time. We walked through the front door of the shelter. We saw no one around, so we headed back to the animal holding area. We could see Hayley and Jennifer, a part-time employee, discussing something that must have been unpleasant for they looked and sounded tense. An older man stood beside them saying nothing. He did not look pleased either. We approached down the center aisle.

"What do you mean he got out?" Hayley asked.

"I told you the fence needed fixing yesterday," Jennifer answered.

"Yeah, and I thought you were going to take care of it!"

"With the holiday, it was hard to find anyone who would come out to fix it."

Jennifer and Hayley saw Todd approaching and Jennifer started to cry before taking off down the hall.

I had a suspicion that it was not good. "What happened?" I asked Hayley.

"There was a weak spot in the fence. I guess Christmas squeezed out. He's gone."

Under the circumstances, I wondered why they were just standing around. "Did you call him? Maybe we can get in the truck and find him."

Hayley shook her head. "Jennifer was so upset, she has been out calling and looking for him since two-thirty. She was afraid to even tell me. He's been gone for hours now. He could be anywhere."

The stranger pushed forward, holding something up. "Excuse me, but is this the missing dog?"

All three of us peered at a photo that he held in his hand. It sure looked like Christmas to me.

"That's Christmas," Todd said immediately.

The man let out a deep sigh. "When he lived with us, we called him Jake. We learned very early on that no fence could hold that dog. When Jake wanted to go, Jake went."

"Jake?" I repeated.

"That was his name when he lived with us." The stranger held out his hand. "Bill Conner."

I shook his hand and introduced myself and Todd. "We adopted him for Christmas and just came in to get him for good. We didn't know he was yours."

"Jake is a bit of a wanderer. I think he goes where he wants to go. When he lived with us he would be gone for a few days, doing Jake business, and then just unexpectedly return."

"He wasn't that way with us," Todd said quickly. "I mean, he stuck around."

Bill Conner put his hands in his pockets and looked at Todd. "As far as him being my dog, nobody owns Jake. Sooner or later, Jake goes where he wants to go. You can't just pick Jake out and think you own him. Jake has to pick you out. That's the way it works with him. It may be that Jake's business is over with both of our families." Bill Conner smiled and shrugged his shoulders as if to say that he was accepting a reality even if he did not like it. "Jake has new Jake business."

We were all silent for a moment until Todd spoke up, seeming slightly offended. "Christmas was a good dog for us."

I considered that to be an enormous understatement.

"I can't tell you how sorry I am," Hayley said. "If Christmas shows up here, I'll call you both and we'll see what we can work out."

Todd reached out and put his hand on Hayley's shoulder and spoke once more as if to reassure us all. "Don't worry. Christmas can take care of himself."

CHAPTER 14

We pulled out of the shelter parking lot to a light snow shower. It was too warm for the snow to stick, but the gray sky set an appropriate backdrop for my disappointment. Todd seemed to know from my silence that I was upset and bothered. He kept saying, "Don't worry, Dad. Christmas will be fine." I was amazed that Todd seemed to be handling this better than me.

When we turned into our driveway after a long and silent trip home, Mary Ann was waiting for us. I dreaded telling her, but when I got out of the truck she just gave me a big hug and said, "I'm sorry, George."

"How did you know?"

"I called the shelter. I wanted to remind you to buy more dog food. I talked to Hayley and she told me."

"It's all right. It's probably for the best," I said. I got the collar, the leash, and the yellow tennis ball out of the back of the truck. "I guess we won't need these anymore." I tossed them on the ground and walked off toward the barn- yard.

Todd started to follow me until Mary Ann called him back. "Todd, why don't you come to the house with me. I think your dad needs a little time to think."

I went into the barn and found the milking stool waiting in my thinking spot.

Mary Ann was right. I had been a fool about this dog. I handled the whole thing poorly. What happened was exactly what I feared, but it was my own fault this time. It was like authoring your own worst nightmare. Everybody has some- thing they aren't very good at and I guess dog relationships just don't work for me. I stared at Tucker's old collar hang- ing on the wall and resolved to toss it into a trash can. I was done with dogs. This time for good.

If Bill Conner was right about this dog, then it might not have mattered. He was destined to drift off anyway. It sounded like he was going to go where he wanted to go. I admired the dog for his independence, but I found it hard to believe that he would have wandered off from this farm. From the beginning, he seemed so comfortable with us and us with him.

I exhaled deeply. On top of everything else, my leg was throbbing in pain. I shifted my weight and tried to get more comfortable when I heard something. *Pong. . . . pong . . . pong.* I was still a little goosey about that cougar, so I tensed up. Before I could place the sound, a yellow tennis ball rolled right up to the foot that was connected to the end of my aching right leg. I was ready to pick it up and throw it right back at Todd.

I turned toward the barn door to throw, but it wasn't Todd. Standing there in the door frame, with the last remnant of sunlight to his back and snowflakes falling over him like a thousand tiny paratroopers, was a dog named Christmas. His tail was wagging and you would have thought that he never left us. I yelled, "Come here, boy! Come on now!" He hesitated for just a second, but then bounded toward me.

Rising off the milk stool when he jumped, I was knocked back onto my own haunches. He was so glad to see me. I hugged him and buried my face in his winter cold, winter clean fur. For a moment, I'm sure my grin was wider than Todd's grin on a spring-painting day, a creek-exploring day, or a radio-listening day. I could not wait to show *my* dog to my son.

Grunting, my stiff leg hindering my ability to stand, I asked, "You want to play catch?" Christmas was wagging his tail. He had clearly chosen us just like we chose him. With all of my strength, I let the ball sail through the barn door and out into the cold winter air. He barked twice and scampered off into the barnyard.

With a second effort, I stood, remembering that for many years my grandfather hung the stool on a nail along the wall. I picked the stool up and turned it over. There was still an old piece of leather strap nailed to the underside. I found the nail and hung the stool up by its strap before heading inside to share my good news with Mary Ann and Todd. I was hoping that it would be a long time before I would need that stool again.

I headed for the back door, yelling, "Mary Ann, Todd, get out here, now!"

Christmas raced around the corner with the ball in his mouth. I tossed the ball again and Christmas disappeared around the side of the barn, out of view.

Mary Ann and Todd opened the door and nearly fell out onto the porch with worry. "What's wrong?" Mary Ann asked.

"I just figured out how to get Christmas back."

"How?" Todd asked.

"It's easy. I'll just throw the ball and he'll fetch it."

"What?" Mary Ann asked.

On cue, Christmas roared around the corner with the ball in his mouth and bounded up onto the porch. I shrugged my shoulders. "See. It worked."

Christmas was home, this time for good. Todd and Mary Ann's reunion with him was no less exciting than my own, although Mary Ann could not resist tugging his ears gently and scolding him for running away. "And to not even leave a note. Shame on you!"

After things settled down, I made a call to Hank, letting him know that it all worked out and to thank him for helping me to set things straight. I got another surprise.

"George," he said, with the confidence I always admired, "I'm not getting any younger, you know."

"I hadn't noticed."

"It's time for me to be thinking about the mark I leave with this life. I just want you to know that I sent a construction company out to the Cherokee County Animal Shelter. That place is a disgrace, but it won't be when I'm done with it."

"Nope, Hank, when you do something, it's done right." So, that explained the construction company trailer in the shelter parking lot. Hank was wasting no time making things right for the dogs of Cherokee County.

Later that night, sitting in front of the dying embers of my fire, I put my newspaper down and closed my eyes. I reached out and stroked my dog's fur, listening with pleasure as his tail thumped the floor. I thought I could almost hear Mary Ann chuckle and say, "And George, when does Christmas end?"

I smiled to myself while still petting the dog, and then whispered to my wife, to my children, and to the whole world, "As long as we can still make room at the inn, Christmas never ends."

During the week of October 17, 2002, a mountain lion was killed on the highway near Kansas City. An expert concluded that it had never lived in captivity. There continue to be numerous sightings in the area.

Acknowledgments

As a novice to the trade, it never occurred to me how much help I would need to reach the end or just how distant that end might be. A book like this does not have one author. Every sentence on every page is a collaboration. This story started almost ten years ago as five typed pages read to my family and shared with a few friends at Christmas. They offered their support and advice, which resulted in a longer version that I read the following holiday. They encouraged me to try to publish it. With the very capable help of Jean Lucas, a local freelance editor, I submitted the story to *Capper's* magazine, and it was published as a short story in the fall of 2003. Several years later, and after writing a full-length novel that's still stuck in a box, I found Jonathan Clements and Taylor Joseph at the Nashville Agency. They thought the story could be marketed as a Christmas gift book. With their guidance, the now-lengthened text traveled to the desk of Andrew Corbin at Doubleday. Andrew was enthusiastic about the story concept from the beginning, but wondered if I could make some revisions. Armed with some of Andrew's very good ideas, I set out again. A month later, I resubmitted to Doubleday and nervously waited for Andrew's call. He got back to me promptly and the conversation went something like, "Love the book, but can you double the length?"

Off to work I went. Fortunately, Andrew enlisted some help for me. In Becky Cabaza, I had a real pro in my corner. Becky took my literary hand and guided me to a final draft. She helped me develop an even better story and mercifully did not require me to add even one more page! To Jean, Jonathan, Taylor, Becky, and all of the other excellent people at Doubleday, many thanks for making this book possible.

As if all this help wasn't enough, other people contributed too. My good friend and law partner, Joe Norton, spent hours reading each version and offering his ideas and support. My dad, Rod Kincaid, and my legal assistant, Martha Huggins, fixed the details that were too often lost on me. Most especially, I want to acknowledge and thank my wife, Michale Ann, for never accepting anything but the best from me.

This story was born from my rural roots on a Kansas farmstead. To those before me who made it possible, my thanks. I hope you, the reader, enjoyed reading this story as much as I enjoyed writing it.

Greg Kincaid
Olathe, Kansas

Special Thanks

I would like to offer a special thanks to the Olathe Animal Shelter and most especially Todd Kuhn, Carol Falkner, and Carol's dog, Maggie. Maggie was a former guest at the shelter and now lives with Carol. I visited several shelters while researching this story and was impressed by the dedication of the employees and the gracious reception I always received from so many fine dogs. To all of the dogs that shared their stories with me, thank you too.

About the Author

GREG KINCAID, when not writing, is a practicing lawyer, specializing in divorce and family law mediation. He lives on a farm in eastern Kansas with his wife, three horses, two dogs, and two cats.